Get Your
Coventry Romances
Home Subscription NOW

And Get These
4 Best-Selling Novels
FREE:

LACEY
by Claudette Williams

THE ROMANTIC WIDOW
by Mollie Chappell

HELENE
by Leonora Blythe

THE HEARTBREAK TRIANGLE
by Nora Hampton

HONORA CLARE

by

Sheila Bishop

FAWCETT COVENTRY • NEW YORK

HONORA CLARE

Published by Fawcett Coventry Books, a unit of CBS Publications, the Consumer Publishing Division of CBS Inc.

ISBN: 0-449-50167-1

Printed in the United States of America

First Fawcett Coventry printing: March 1981

10 9 8 7 6 5 4 3 2 1

CONTENTS

PART ONE

A Good Idea

"You will wish to sell the property in Bath, my dear Honora," said Mr. Sydney Clare, standing in front of the library fire. "You had better let me instruct the lawyers on your behalf."

His cousin thanked him and said she would think it over. She disliked being called Honora, her name was invariably shortened to Honor.

"I should prefer to have a look at the houses before I make up my mind," she added after a moment.

"What good will that do? You can hardly go and live in one of them. And we have both told you already, you must look on Walbury as your home."

As Honor had spent the whole twenty-four years of her life at Walbury, she took a rather ironic view of his generosity. Then she recognized that it was a genuine offer and more than she was entitled to. Walbury Park had been in the Clare family for six generations, but the property was entailed, and when her father died it had passed to his nearest male heir, since Honor, his only child, was a mere female. The Sidney Clares had a perfect right to be here and they were under no obligation to let her remain. They had been kind enough to offer her a home and it was a pity that she did not like them. She had been more or less bound to accept, because she had nowhere else to go. She murmured something grateful.

"You will have to learn to make yourself useful," said Mrs. Sidney Clare. She was sitting bolt upright, stabbing away with her needle at some horrid, scratchy garment obviously intended for the poor. "I shall require you to assist with the children and so forth."

"Of course, Cousin Euphemia. I shall be glad to help in any way I can."

Did the woman expect her to lie on a sofa all day, reading novels? Perhaps she did. The Sidney Clares had come from the genteel trivialities of a London suburb and had no idea how one lived on a country estate. Honor was prepared to show them. As for helping with the children, that would not be very hard work. There were only two little girls and they were in the capable care of their governess, Miss Fielder. Among all the newcomers at Walbury, Miss Fielder was the one person Honor liked and could talk to as a kindred spirit.

She looked round the dear old library with its tiers of well-read books rising to the ceiling, and at the crimson damask curtains and matching chairs, all a little faded now but still so cheerful and friendly. The apple logs hissed in the grate. She knew the tree they came from, remembered the day it had to be felled. Sidney knew nothing as yet, standing there pink and plump, trying to look as though he owned the place—which was rather pathetic, considering that he actually did. Sidney would not be so bad without his wife.

Cousin Euphemia had a pursed-up mouth and sandy eyelashes. She was a Scot. Not that Honor had anything against the Scots, she had always

8

thought them a most interesting and romantic nation, until she met Cousin Euphemia.

"When you write to this lawyer," the lady said to her husband, "you must be sure to point out that his letter was wrongly directed."

This surprised both Sidney and Honor.

"Wrongly directed, my love, what do you mean?"

"It was addressed to Miss Clare."

"But I am Miss Clare," said Honor.

"Not now. You were entitled to use that form in your father's lifetime, but on his death you became merely Miss Honora. Effie is now Miss Clare, the eldest daughter of the present head of the family."

Effie was nine years old.

"My dear cousin, I do apologize! You are perfectly right to insist on Effie's taking precedence over me. She should be taught to know her proper place. It is a thing some people never seem to learn, and they generally end by making themselves ridiculous."

Honor got up swiftly and left the room, before Euphemia had time to perceive the insult she had wrapped up so carefully.

She stood in the hall, raging. Head of the family, indeed! You'd think Sidney was an earl at least. Why had they moved the table in here? It looked quite absurd, and so did that simpering statue they brought with them from Hackney.

She had meant to go and sit in her dressing room, then she remembered how cold it would be, now that fires upstairs were forbidden. She could have endured that, only the maids would insist on lighting an illicit one for her, which might get them into trouble with their new mistress. Honor was finding it quite difficult to prevent the servants' taking foolish risks because of their fondness for her. She decided to go for a walk.

Muffled in an old cloak that had seen better days, she set out to brave the biting February cold and, if possible, walk off her bad temper. She was a tall, slender young woman, with regular features, a mouth that was too wide for beauty, and the vivid coloring—black hair and blue eyes—that she had inherited from her Irish mother.

Walbury Park was in Oxfordshire, an Elizabethan house set in a beautiful amphitheatre of grass and trees. Honor glanced back with affection at the long, low building, so exactly suited to be the home of an ancient but untitled family who had never given themselves airs, while always living in a style of unaffected elegance. That stupid couple thought it would look better with a row of arcaded pillars and a portico; she had heard them say so. If only Papa had not died.

He had been dead for three months. The worst of her grief was over, because he had been a helpless invalid for two years, and for the last part of that time he was so ill that she could only be thankful when death released him. So that in a sense her mourning was an old wound and recovery was in sight. All the time he was ill they had known, of course, that she would eventually lose Walbury, that it must go to those distant cousins he had never cared for. At that point, luckily for Mr. Clare's peace of mind, he had imagined that he was leaving her fairly well provided for. There had been a good deal of money that was not included in the settled estate. But when the will came to be read, most of this had vanished in a bank failure, or been muddled away by the lawyers or spent. Honor had to admit that Papa had always been extravagant, though she had been too young and lighthearted to realize it. All she had inherited was a very tiny capital sum and two houses in Bath which had once belonged to an aunt. They stood side by side in a place called Belmont and had been let for some years. Now they were empty and Sidney wanted her to sell them.

Was this the wisest thing to do? She would have a little more money, but she had already decided that no sum of money was going to be of the slightest use to her unless it was large enough to set her up in a home of her own, far away from Sidney and Euphemia. Would the houses in Belmont produce enough? Suppose she was to sell one and live in the other? She wished she had someone to consult. She had not realized until her father was taken ill how isolated they were here, surrounded by other even larger estates, with everyone living a fair distance apart. Their nearest neighbors had been close friends whom she could have relied on for good advice, but they had let their house and moved away after the only son of the family had been killed at Waterloo.

All this time she had been walking round the lake. It was a pretty stretch of ornamental water, artificially contrived, with a bridge leading on to a small island where there was a miniature temple—an enchanted scene, even today in the muted light and cold stillness of February. For once Honor was not in the mood to appreciate it.

She had nearly completed the circuit when she saw a figure coming towards her. It was Miss Fielder, the children's governess, a quiet, clever woman of about thirty. Honor thought she must be deep in some kind of intellectual abstraction.

11

As they met she called out a greeting, but Miss Fielder hastened on, stooping and stumbling as though she hardly knew where she was. Honor paused, waiting for the children to appear; Effie, the reigning Miss Clare, and her younger sister Letty. There was no sign of them. This was rather extraordinary. If she had been a different sort of woman and if this had been a warm day in June, one would suspect an assignation. Neither Miss Fielder nor the weather suggested the pleasures of dalliance. Without knowing why she did so, Honor turned back and followed her over the bridge.

Halfway across, she paused, not wishing to pry. Then she heard the sound of desperate sobs coming from the temple. She hurried inside.

The governess was huddled on one of the stone benches, crying wretchedly and shaking, either from cold or fear or both.

"Miss Fielder, what is the matter?"

Miss Fielder looked up, choking back her tears.

"Oh, Miss Clare! I beg your pardon—such a stupid weakness—"

"Is there nothing I can do for you? Won't you tell me what is wrong?"

"I—I've been dismissed. They are sending me away next week."

"Good heavens, why?"

Lucy Fielder blew her nose. She was thin and sallow, not at all pretty, but with large brown eyes that were generally full of intelligent interest in the world around her and a confiding wish to share her enjoyment with others.

"Mrs. Clare disapproves of my owning a copy of *The Rights of Women*."

"What a bigot she is! I have never read the book

12

myself, but I believe Mary Wollstonecraft had some most striking ideas."

"I should never have quoted any of them to Effie or Letty, even if they had been old enough to understand—which of course they are not. And I don't know why Mrs. Clare has suddenly decided that I am so very much in the wrong, for I had the book lying on a shelf in my room, quite openly, all the time I was with them at Hackney. Perhaps I have displeased her in some other way."

Light was beginning to dawn.

"You need not search your conscience. You are being got rid of because she has found a cheaper substitute."

Miss Fielder did not think this was likely.

"My salary is very modest."

"I can believe you. But she is obliged to give you something. She would not have to pay me a penny."

"*You*, Miss Clare? Surely she does not expect—you cannot be made into the children's governess?"

"Why not? Do you think I am too flighty?"

Honor laughed, in spite of her indignation, and sat down on the stone bench.

"You are a lady!" said Miss Fielder.

"So are you. We are both the daughters of gentlemen who have left us rather ill provided for. I am not too proud to take care of my little cousins, only I will not let myself be used in such a nasty, mean, penny-pinching scheme, and I shall tell Mrs. Clare so directly I see her. There is no question of your being sent away, so don't torment yourself. I am quite disgusted with her behavior and I shall tell her that too."

"Please don't," said Miss Fielder quickly. "You

13

must not say anything on my account, I beg you not to. It will make no difference. She will only punish me by being crosser than ever an she will not keep me on."

Thinking it over, Honor decided reluctantly that this was probably true, because once Miss Fielder was out of the way, once the little girls had no one to teach and supervise them, it would be much easier for Euphemia to shame or coerce Honor into doing what was required of her. It would be difficult to refuse such essential duties while she was living on her cousins' charity. If she did go on refusing, Euphemia might eventually give in and engage another governess, but it would be someone new, not poor Lucy Fielder.

"Where will you go?" she asked with anxious compassion. "Have you any family?"

"I have a brother who is a curate in Yorkshire. And my sister is a governess in Kensington. Neither of them can take me in. I have a friend who lets lodgings in Bath; of course she cannot afford to take me for nothing, but I have saved some money and she will charge me as little as she can.... Yes, I had best go to Bath, it is a good place to be. I can apply to an agency there, or advertise."

She spoke quite jauntily now, almost managing to hide the tremor in her voice, and the note of deep apprehension.

"Do you know your way about in Bath?" asked Honor. "Have you ever been in a street called Belmont?"

"Belmont? That is on the Lansdown Road, the first or second terrace on the right as you begin to climb the hill."

"I have some property there which I want to see before I decide whether to sell it or not." An idea

14

was shaping in her mind. "Do you think, if I came to Bath with you next week, your friend would be able to let me have a room for a night or two?"

"I am sure she would be delighted, Miss Clare. Though I am afraid it will not be quite what you are used to: Monmouth Street, not a very grand address."

"I shall not be a very grand visitor. I am not going to Bath to enjoy myself, or even to take the waters. I simply want to look at two empty houses and consult a lawyer."

She made the same announcement to her cousins after dinner. Of course Euphemia objected. It was out of the question for her to stay with the governess at a common lodging house! What would people say?

"I expect they will say that Cousin Sidney ought to have escorted me himself. Then we could have put up at the White Hart, which I understand is the best hotel."

Honor took a wicked pleasure in saying this, though she did not at all want Sidney's company in Bath. She would be far happier with Lucy Fielder.

Sidney had the grace to look a little uncomfortable.

"I am sorry, it is not convenient for me to leave Walbury at present. If you are set on going to Bath, I am sure you will be quite safe with Miss Fielder and her friends. They may not be people of fashion but I have no doubt they are perfectly respectable."

His wife attacked him on this subject when Honor had gone to bed.

"What are you thinking of? How can you let

her go careering off to Bath with a person like Fielder?"

"My dear Euphemia, I can't prevent her. She has got it into her head that I am not going to handle this business properly, though I don't know whether she distrusts my probity or simply my judgment. She is determined to look into things for herself. She is twenty-four years old, she has control of her own money, such as it is—at least she can afford to spend a few days in Bath, and if she is with Miss Fielder she will have the benefit of a chaperone, which removes the only serious objection to her going. In any case, I can't stop her."

(2)

On their first morning in Bath, Lucy meant to call at an agency she knew of, where she said governesses were supplied to the nobility and gentry. On her way she took Honor to Gay Street to keep an appointment with a lawyer named French. Honor had never been to Bath before (her father had not cared for watering places) and the cold, bright morning was just right for a first view of the city. As they walked up into Queen Square she could feel her spirits rising at the sight of those four ranges of lofty houses facing each other across the great quadrangle. She was reminded of some ordered and stately piece of music, by Handel perhaps. They turned into Gay Street, and Lucy left her at Mr. French's door.

Honor had never met Mr. French. He was not her family lawyer, he had acted for the late owner of the Bath property, Honor's aunt—or to be more accurate, the widow of her uncle, her father's

16

brother, Philip Clare. He and his wife, having no children, had left the houses to Honor.

Mr. French turned out to be a pleasant, astute-looking man of about forty.

"I am very pleased to meet you, Miss Clare," he said. "It is much easier to deal directly instead of continually writing letters. I gather you want to look over the house in Belmont?"

"If you please. There are two houses, are there not?" she asked, a little anxiously, for she was counting on that.

"Yes and no," said Mr. French, being lawyerlike and ambiguous, she thought. "That is to say there *were* two houses, standing side by side. They were bought as an investment—Mrs. Philip Clare never lived there—and one was let to a man who took in boarders. Everyone in Bath does that. After a while he asked if he might rent the second house, open a doorway through the partition wall on each floor and double his number of lodgers. That is how things have been left. It is at present one house, but of course the doors can be blocked at any time, dividing it back into the original two."

"I had thought of selling one of the houses and living in the other."

Mr. French raised no objection until he grasped the fact that she was hoping to live on the proceeds of the sale, with very little else to support her.

"I don't think you could manage, ma'am," he said in a rather shocked voice, scribbling down figures and clicking his teeth. "The capital sum you might obtain would hardly yield a sufficient income."

"I thought houses in Bath always fetched such a good price."

"Times are changing. The number of visitors

17

has declined ever since sea bathing became popular. That's why your former tenant didn't wish to renew his lease. The city is still enlarging but the families who come here now wish to settle as permanent residents."

"Then why shouldn't I sell to one of them?"

"The Lansdown Road is inclined to be noisy, so near the hub of activity. Ideal for a short stay, but people who come here to live want the greater peace and space of the New Town—across the river in Bathwick, you know."

Honor did not know and had nothing to say.

"Don't misunderstand me, Miss Clare. You could certainly sell either or both your houses, but I must warn you not to be too ambitious over the price." After a short pause, he said, "Shall we go round there now? It is quite close."

They walked up hill into the Circus. Honor had seen prints of this famous ring of thirty houses, but found them astonishing all the same. They turned into Bennet Street and Mr. French pointed out the Upper Rooms, a rather squat building erected a generation earlier. Bennet Street was wide but not long, crossed at the end by the busy thoroughfare that climbed up to Lansdown.

"There are your houses," said Mr. French. "Do you like them?"

"Where?"

"Straight ahead of us on the high pavement."

On the far side of the Lansdown Road the pavement was so high that it had to be reached by a flight of steps, and a railing ran along the top to prevent anyone's falling over. The houses that rose above this escarpment stood out on the skyline looking inaccessibly tall. This dramatic height

18

added something unusual to their classical elegance. Honor felt a sudden pride of ownership.

There were twenty-six houses in Belmont and hers were more or less in the middle, so that they faced down the opening of Bennet Street. One of the two front doors had a look of being permanently disused. Mr. French took out a key to unlock the other, standing on a little platform of shallow steps. Beside the door Honor noticed a small round window with glazing bars set like the spokes in a wheel.

They went in. It was dark at first, after the sharp light outside, and there was a musty, dusty smell. Honor had never been in an empty house and she was affected by a sense of neglect and desolation, and the ghosts of old picture frames on the faded wallpaper. Then they walked through to the back, to a larger room with windows facing east which got the morning sun. She went to look out. There was a tiny garden, which she hadn't expected, and there were more houses and streets beyond. Because the ground fell away, the prospect was quite open, there was none of the usual town feeling of being shut in.

Mr. French took her all round, pointing out steps, cupboards, cellars, attics, pretty cornices, creaking floorboards, advantages and disadvantages. Each house in Belmont had five floors including a basement, each floor had two rooms, the one at the front being smaller because of the space taken up by the hall passage and staircase. Because of the communicating doors on every floor, Honor's two had indeed been converted into one house with four rooms at each level.

I should like to live here, she thought, in a house of my own, as different as possible from Walbury,

19

away from Sidney and Euphemia and the horrid things they are doing there. But what was the use? She couldn't afford it and even one of the houses would be too big for her.

When Mr. French had finished taking her round she wanted to linger. So she made a grateful little speech, and told him she must not waste any more of his time, she would return the key in a day or so. He took the hint and left her alone. If he thought she was mad, he was too polite to show it.

When he had gone, she became fascinated by the little round window next to the front door. She stood looking through it at her circular picture of Bath, and presently she saw Lucy Fielder walking along Belmont and studying the houses as she passed.

Honor opened the front door. "Have you come to call on me?"

"Oh, is this your house? I was trying to guess which it could be. How lucky to have the view along Bennet Street to the Circus."

"Do come inside. How did your inquiries go?"

"Not very well. They have nothing to offer me at present."

Lucy changed the subject and began to admire the house. Her enthusiasm was quite untouched by envy. She had heard Honor's hopeful schemes and presently asked what Mr. French had thought of them.

"He said I should not get a big enough price. It seems that houses in Belmont are not in demand at present."

"Like governesses," said Lucy.

She managed a laugh which sounded as though it hurt her throat.

Honor said, "We've been long enough in these unheated rooms. Let's go."

They had meant to take a stroll round the city to admire the sights but they both felt too cold and decided to go back to Monmouth Street. There would be a long wait before dinner, so they went into a pastry-cook's, where Honor bought some slices of ham and two cream tarts. She had brought a canister of tea with her, and they had a picnic lunch in her room, in front of a bright coal fire, with no Euphemia to disapprove.

The glowing warmth and the taste of sweetness revived and comforted them both, and they were quite cheerful for a time, but gradually they became silent, each with her own unhappy thoughts. Honor dreaded going back to Walbury and was ashamed of this because Lucy had cried at being sent away. Treated worse than a servant, she had still wanted to stay. The alternative was so grim.

Lucy stared into the fire, brooding. "I wonder if I could get a post in a school."

"How would that compare with being in a private family?"

"A friend of mine says it's worse. You are still at the mercy of another woman's whims, the work is harder (more children to look after) and the food is probably not so good. Of course I am speaking of what it is to be a junior teacher. To have one's own school would be entirely different. The woman who can afford that has an uncommon degree of independence. She may work hard, but she can direct everything the way she chooses, and besides that she is the mistress of her own home."

It was then that Honor had her inspiration.

"Why should we not open a school? The house in Belmont would be ideal for the purpose. We'll go into partnership and the fees will bring in a good income for us both."

Lucy gazed at her.

"You cannot be serious?" she said doubtfully.

"Yes, I am. Why not? Please don't tell me I'm too much of a lady. We must get rid of these delusions of grandeur—I mean your delusions about my grandeur. If we are to be partners—"

"How can we? You know I haven't any money!"

"That doesn't matter. No, don't argue, Lucy—listen! You have been a governess, I have just become a poor relation. Keeping a school is the only way that women like us can escape from a life of slavery in other women's houses. I could never undertake such a venture on my own, I have no previous experience and I should never be clever enough to teach subjects like arithmetic or geography. But you know all about such things. The serious instruction will be your contribution; mine will be the house and the money that is needed to set us up. And I could give simple lessons, such as writing and drawing. You could manage without me, but I certainly could not manage without you. Surely you can see that?"

"A share in a school—I never dreamed of such a chance coming my way. But could we succeed? Where should we find our pupils?"

"We must have cards printed and send them out to everyone we know."

In their enthusiasm they borrowed the Bath Guide from their landlady so that they could study the scholastic announcements there. Presently Lucy began to scribble a tentative draft. She showed Honor the result.

Belmont   Bath
Young Ladies Educated in the Care of
Miss Honora Clare and Miss Lucy Fielder
Board and Tuition including:
History Geography Arithmetic and French
Writing Drawing Music and Dancing
Additional Visits by the most Approved
Masters if desired
Two Vacations a Year of One month each

"I'm not sure whether we should print the fee
when we've decided on it. And I've left out needlework; that will have to go in somewhere."

"It looks very impressive," said Honor.

PART TWO

Not Such a Good Idea

Sidney and Euphemia were outraged by the news that a cousin of theirs was proposing to keep a school; they washed their hands of her. Honor did not care, she had done with Sidney and Euphemia.

She applied to Mr. French, who was helpful in recommending tradesmen, including a printer. The cards were soon ready, she was secretly elated to read her own name in print and sat down to write to all the friends and acquaintances belonging to her social, carefree life before her father had been taken ill.

There were normally two school terms in the year; the longer ran from February to the end of July, the shorter from September to Christmas. This year, however, Honor and Lucy had decided that they did not want to wait until the autumn before beginning their great venture—in fact they could hardly afford to—so Honor told everyone that they would be ready to receive their first pupils directly after Easter.

There was a great deal to be done while waiting for the applications to come in, and Honor and Lucy were so busy and happy spurring on the painters and paperhangers, visiting cabinetmakers, upholsterers and china warehouses, ordering books and engaging servants, that they hardly felt a pang of disappointment when the answers to Honor's letters began to arrive. Some admired her enterprise, some gloomily prophesied disaster, very few of them actually knew of any real flesh-and-blood little girl who needed educating.

"It seems rather extraordinary," said Honor, "considering how many families one knows who seem to be afflicted with far too many daughters."

They told each other they must not be impatient, went on moving the furniture about and putting up pictures, and then suddenly it was April, the school was due to open in a week, and after all Honor's efforts only two pupils were expected, Nancy Newlander and Evelina Rose.

"And what can we say to those two, or their parents, when they arrive? Who ever heard of a school with two teachers and two pupils! What are we to do? What ought we to have done?"

"It might have made a difference," said Lucy, "if we'd been in time to get an advertisement in this year's *Bath Directory*."

"We didn't want to advertise," Honor reminded her. "We were going to be so select. Well, that's just what we shall be, isn't it? Exclusive to the last degree."

She stood by her writing table in the pretty little front parlor and looked through the open door into one of the schoolrooms. The large circular table had a cherry red cloth, the straight, neat chairs were all new and unscratched, a terrestrial globe stood in the window. She liked the smell of fresh paint and the flowery wallpaper, though her renovations had cost more than she expected, and she knew she ought not to have bought such an expensive pianoforte.

How was she going to pay for everything if the school didn't succeed? We must succeed, she told herself fiercely; given the pupils, there was not the smallest reason why they should fail. They had not cast their net quite wide enough, that was all. It would still be possible to advertise in the newspapers, but she thought that frankly vulgar, as though one was throwing the place open to all comers. Surely there were more discreet ways of making the school's existence known.

Lucy had a letter from her sister, and she went upstairs to read it. Honor opened a drawer and helped herself to a handful of their printed cards; presently she left the house and started down into the city. She was making for the Pump Room, which stood in the Abbey Churchyard, at right angles to the high, perpendicular Abbey, where the west front was covered with angels, climbing up and down Jacob's Ladder in a perpetuity of stone. The Bath season was nearly over, but there was still a fair number of people visible through the tall windows of the Pump Room, walking and talking and drinking the statutory glasses of disagreeable warm water. Honor went in. She strolled as far as the embrasure that overlooked the King's Bath, green and enclosed under its faint veil of steam. She glanced around as though searching for a friend. No one seemed to be watching her. It was a chilly spring morning, so she had been able to carry a muff. She withdrew one gloved hand, surreptitiously laid down several of the cards on a nearby table, and moved quietly away.

After leaving the Pump Room, she visited four of the circulating libraries and planted a few of her cards in each. People who frequented libraries must be fond of reading and would want their daughters to be properly educated. She went home, pleased with her morning's work but slightly embarrassed, and decided not to tell Lucy about it.

Lucy had news of her own.

"What do you think my sister says in her letter? She has a pupil for us. A little girl called Sally Colvin; it seems she is an orphan who has been living with her aunt. The aunt is expecting to be married, so Sally is to go to school."

The aunt, a Miss Butley, was a friend of the Robinsons, who employed Mary Fielder as a governess. Mrs. Robinson was prepared to recommend "any school that is kept by a sister of our Miss Fielder." It was all most satisfactory—an omen of better things.

Two days later they received some visitors. They were in the ground floor schoolroom, unpacking a parcel of stationery, when their newly appointed parlormaid announced: "Mr. and Mrs. Marlow and the Misses Marlow."

The room seemed to fill with people; a tall man, a rather sweet-looking woman with a tired, anxious expression, and three—actually three—girls of the age to need educating.

"Miss Clare?" began the lady, looking at Lucy.

"No, I am Miss Fielder, ma'am. This is Miss Clare."

"Oh, I beg your pardon. But you do keep a school, do you not? We understood—" She hesitated, apparently taking in the fresh, glossy look of the house, and the complete stillness.

"Our school is so new," said Honor, "that we don't open for another week."

27

"Oh dear, what a pity. We are in such a hurry, you see. We came to Bath to inspect another establishment, but it didn't suit. They cannot accept all three of our girls and we don't wish them to be separated. One separation is bad enough: my husband and I are sailing for India almost immediately."

"Perhaps you still have some vacancies?" suggested Mr. Marlow.

Honor agreed that they had, and then said, in the manner of someone making a concession, "If it is a matter of urgency, there is no real reason why your daughters should not come to us straight away. Provided you approve of the school itself. Perhaps you would like to see round."

Mrs. Marlow was volubly grateful; it was soon clear that she was going to approve of everything...

"French!" she exclaimed in wonder, as though they were offering to teach Chinese. "And these pretty bedrooms, everything so nice and new... I am glad the school is going to be rather small, it will be more homey for our girls. I have never left them before, Miss Clare. It has all been so difficult. My husband has been offered this important appointment on condition that we sail immediately. I was in despair until we went into Meyler's Library to consult the newspapers and found your card."

Mr. Marlow asked whether they would make a reduction in the fees. It was usual, he said, when there were several children from the same family. Honor was quite ready to agree.

Lucy had taken the girls under her wing. They were called Martha, Margaret and Marianne, aged fourteen, eleven and seven, and all had a distinct likeness to each other and to their mother. They had straight, brown hair and light blue eyes. Martha and Margaret were grave and silent, watching their parents as though they expected them to vanish. Little Marianne ran from room to room; it was a beautiful house and she was sure she would like to come and live here.

Everything was settled. The Marlows would stay at the Christopher for one more night; the girls and their baggage would be deposited at Belmont the following day before their parents drove to Bristol.

"I can't believe it!" said Lucy when they were alone. "Are we dreaming? How did they come to hear of us? I did not follow something Mrs. Marlow said about Meyler's Library."

Rather guiltily, Honor explained.

"How clever of you!" said Lucy admiringly. "I should never have thought of that."

The young Marlows arrived next day as arranged. It was a doleful occasion, the whole family, including Mr. Marlow, had evidently been crying. He pressed a bundle of banknotes into Honor's hand, which took her by surprise. She did not know if she was supposed to count them. Mrs. Marlow presented her with a letter which, she said, contained "everything you need to know."

The final farewells were mercifully short, as the carriage was waiting. After her parents had driven away, eleven-year-old Margaret said, "We may never see them again. Why did they have to go?"

"You know they told us why," said her elder sister Martha. "Papa's situation. It was absolutely necessary. And of course they will come back."

Reality suddenly broke on little Marianne. She

closed her eyes, opened her mouth and bellowed, "I want my Mama!"

During the next few days Honor felt less like a schoolmistress than an indulgent aunt, inventing treats and distractions. The Marlows were nice, well-behaved girls but they were very unhappy, and no wonder. Anyone who went to India was bound to be away at least two or three years. Mrs. Marlow's letter was rather pathetic, full of little, useless pieces of information as though in writing it she was trying to establish something familiar in her daughters' new surroundings. Not only their birthdays were given but the dates and places of their baptism (the Marlows had moved around a good deal, Honor noticed), a record of all their childish ailments and various motherly anecdotes. Only one thing was missing. There was no list of addresses: neither the parents' destination in India nor the name of any relative in England. In her hurry and distress Mrs. Marlow must have forgotten this. Martha is sure to know, Honor decided. I'll ask her in a week or so.

The day the school opened in earnest the Marlows became quite excited. So did Honor and Lucy, though they felt obliged to assume an air of great calm and experience. The first arrival was Sally Colvin, accompanied by her aunt, Miss Butley.

Sally was an engaging little person, small for nine years old but sturdy and lively. She gazed about her with bright-eyed curiosity, and was quite ready to kiss her aunt goodbye and join Margaret Marlow, who was arranging some books on a shelf in the schoolroom.

"It is all a novelty to her," commented Honor, feeling the aunt might be a little hurt; "I expect she enjoys the company of other children."

Miss Butley was a pale, solid woman whose dress looked expensive and dowdy at the same time. Her manner was slightly defensive, though Honor guessed that this was unusual.

"Other children," she repeated, taking the cue. "Yes, to be sure: that is exactly what Sally needs. It has not been good for her to be so much alone. I promised my dear sister I would keep her with me—what else could I do? She was on her death-bed, and there was not another soul in the world who cared what became of the poor child—but this did not mean she must never be sent away to school."

"Of course not, ma'am. And you will have her with you during the holidays."

Miss Butley said firmly that this would be a great consolation to her.

An hour later there was some confusion when four people were shown into the parlor at the same time. A harassed gentleman leading by the hand an odd-looking, shapeless child, an elderly woman of the housekeeper class and the prettiest little golden-haired sylph Honor had ever seen. This, surely, must be the romantically-named Evelina Rose.

But it was the harassed gentleman who said, "I am Mr. Rose and this is my daughter. Make your curtsy, my dear."

The shapeless child ducked her head. She looks quite half-witted, thought Honor in dismay, though she smiled a welcome.

"We are very glad to see you, Evelina. And this must be Nancy Newlander?"

"I am Corisande Bilting," announced the sylph in a clear, piping voice.

The elderly woman held out a letter. "Mrs. Bilting asked me to give you this, ma'am."

Lucy was taking charge of the Roses. Honor opened the letter. It was written from an address in Hertford Street, just off Park Lane, on expensive paper and in an elegant, if rather florid hand. The writer had heard of the school through a friend, and wished to entrust her precious child to Miss Clare. A banker's draft was enclosed.

So now their numbers were up to seven. It was quite a triumph after the fears of a week ago.

Corisande was an acquisition and helped to compensate for some misgivings over Evelina, who certainly was very odd. By supper time the other girls were shyly making friends, the young Marlows acting almost like hostesses, but Evelina just sat blinking myopically and contributing nothing. Until she suddenly toppled sideways off her chair and lay on the ground without moving.

"Is she dead?" asked Marianne hopefully.

Evelina came round quite quickly. "Did I go off?" she asked.

"There's nothing to be afraid of," said Honor kindly. She was kneeling on the floor, bathing the child's forehead with a damp handkerchief. "You have been overtired by your journey."

"I often go off. Papa says to take no notice." It was the longest speech she had yet made.

"Was it some kind of fit?" Honor asked Lucy afterwards.

"Petit mal, I should think."

"Did her father give you any warning?"

"No. He wouldn't, you know," said Lucy, with an unexpected touch of cynicism. "Parents are ashamed of a child like that. First they try to pretend there's nothing wrong, and then they pack her off to school to be out of sight. Poor little creature."

"But that is quite abominable! And such a responsibility for us. I almost wish—good heavens, who can that be at the door at this hour?"

In the excitement they had forgotten that Nancy Newlander was still to come. When the door opened, a liveried coachman dumped a trunk in the passage and vanished into the gloom. The girl who stood beside the trunk might be only thirteen, but she was nearly as tall as Honor, angular and slouching. Her sullen face was shuttered under frowning black eyebrows.

"Papa's coachman couldn't find the way to Belmont," she remarked in a disparaging voice. "We never thought it would be in the Lansdown Road."

"Well, you are rather late, but never mind. Did no one come with you in the carriage?"

"Lord, no! They're sick of taking me to school. I've been to five in the last two years."

Honor and Lucy exchanged apprehensive glances.

The next few days were extremely exhausting. This was natural enough, it was bound to take some time to assess the abilities of seven unknown girls of such different ages. Sally, Corisande and the three Marlows were all amenable and anxious to do their best. Evelina, to put it bluntly, was almost an idiot. She did what she was told, as far as she was able, but she could neither read or write. It was difficult to know what to do with her. She had to be watched carefully because of her propensity for Going Off. Honor had begun to think of this performance in capital letters; it happened about once a day, and they were afraid of her falling downstairs or setting herself on fire by knocking over a candle.

However, it was Nancy who really overshadowed all their efforts and threatened their good intentions. Insolent and hostile, she was a thoroughly disruptive influence. She boasted of the five schools that had given her up as a bad job, she tried to impress the other girls with her wickedness, and teased poor witless Evelina.

"You aren't going to get any pudding, you're too fat," she said, at the dinner table.

Evelina believed her and began to blubber. Food was her chief pleasure.

"Don't be so unkind to her," said Lucy.

Nancy paid no attention. She whisked a slice of apple pie off Evelina's plate.

Honor put down her spoon. "If you won't behave properly, you can leave the room. Go and stand outside the door."

Still, Nancy paid no attention. Honor got up, caught her by the shoulders and literally dragged her out of the dining room. It was quite a struggle, for Nancy made herself a dead-weight.

Out in the passage, panting a little from her exertions, Honor said, "I don't know why you are determined to be such a nuisance. If you think this is the quickest way of getting yourself sent away from yet another school, let me tell you that we shall not give in so easily."

"You can't afford to, can you? You've got so few girls, you're afraid to lose one."

Honor was so angry that she gave Nancy a ringing slap on the cheek, and was immediately ashamed of having lost her temper.

Nancy winced, but looked rather pleased, as though she knew she had scored a point. And she clearly enjoyed setting a bad example to the other girls. Margaret Marlow was excited by her exploits and was, herself, verging on impertinence.

"I wonder you are able to be so naughty," Honor heard her whispering to Nancy later.

"I'm not afraid of anything they can do to me. I'm not afraid of anyone. At Miss Birkin's, I was caned in front of the whole school. I didn't care."

"I shouldn't like to be caned," remarked the fastidious Corisande.

"You won't be, my dear little sugar mouse. They haven't got a cane, and if they had, they'd never dare to use it."

"I have a very good mind to go out and buy one!" said Honor wrathfully, reporting this to Lucy.

"You don't mean it, Honor? You know we agreed that children ought not to be treated so barbarously."

"I'd make an exception for that young vixen, if I thought it would do any good. Only I don't."

Some instinct told Honor that Nancy was one of those rare people who would willingly endure pain and punishment for the sake of all the trouble they could cause to everyone else, the turmoil and notoriety. It must take a degree of raw physical stoicism; she was pretty sure Nancy had that, and the idea of disgrace meant nothing to her. She was too much at odds with the world to want the world's approval. Why a thirteen-year-old girl should feel like this was a mystery. How they were to keep her in order was a greater mystery still.

On Sunday, Honor and Lucy shepherded their little flock down Guinea Lane and across the London Road to Walcot Parish Church. There were several other schools there, all much larger than theirs. Having no reserved pew they sat a long way back. Honor kept Evelina beside her and prayed fervently that she wouldn't Go Off during the sermon. This prayer, at least, was granted.

Sunday afternoon had been set aside for the girls to write letters home. Sally and Corisande settled down with pens and paper, and so, rather unexpectedly, did Nancy. Lucy was going to write a letter for Evelina.

Martha said, "Who are we to write to, Miss Clare? Papa and Mama are at sea. They won't be in India for several months."

"You can write to them just the same. Your letters will follow on the next boat, and they will be glad to receive them so soon after they arrive."

"We don't know where they are going . . . Papa said they would have to let us know, once they got there . . ."

But that may take more than a year, thought Honor, allowing for the Marlows to reach India, and for their first letter to come home. There was no sense in pointing this out, so she merely said, "Perhaps you would like to write to some of your relations in England instead."

"I don't think we have any."

"I see . . . Martha, did your mother leave any list of addresses with you? Of friends who might be interested to have news of how you are all going on?"

"No, I'm afraid not, Miss Clare." Martha looked awkward and miserable, as though she knew very well that there was something strange about this.

"Well, it doesn't signify. What you and Margaret can do on Sunday afternoons is to write diaries. You can put down everything interesting that has happened in the past week. And as Marianne doesn't write very easily yet, she can do the illustrations."

Marianne was delighted. Martha and Margaret sat mute and unhappy; Honor was very sorry for them.

It had just dawned on her, and perhaps it had dawned on them already, that they had been more or less abandoned on her doorstep like foundlings. Their father had paid for half a year's board and tuition, but that money would be gone long before they could hope to hear from him again. Who would pay next term's fees, or buy any new clothes they needed? Where were they to go in the summer vacation? Who was to be notified in case of serious illness? I ought to have been more practical, thought Honor, only it was all such a rush. Could the Marlows have gone off deliberately without leaving proper directions? Surely not. It was too horrible to contemplate, and that woman loved her children. And her husband was supposed to have some important appointment in India— only that was suspicious too, because if he had a definite appointment, they must have known where they were going.

She sat brooding in a cloud of uncertainty, from which she had to rouse herself when she saw that Sally and Corisande had finished writing. She looked over their letters, interested in neatness and spelling rather than censorship, though she was pleased to find that they had both written happily about life at school.

She did not think Nancy would wish her letter to be read, and was rather surprised when it was laid before her with a defiant flourish. It was atrociously written, much worse than nine-year-old Sally's. Nancy had been so busy creating havoc in all those different schools that she seemed to have avoided learning much at any of them. Her letter was an arresting composition all the same.

Dear Papa and Mana,

This is a stupid scool, wors than the others. There are only six girls hear one has fitts. Miss Feeder is an Old Maid. Miss C fancys she is pritty. She has a Revoltronary book called the Rites of Wumman, I dont think I shd be at a scool were the Teecher is a revlushonary.

Your affec. dauter

Nancy

Honor stared down at the smudged scrawl. She felt her anger surge up as the blood rose into her cheeks. Miss C fancies she is pretty indeed! Impudent little hussy. More serious was the knowledge that although Nancy was nearly illiterate, she had been sharp enough to notice Lucy's copy of Mary Wollstonecraft's famous book lying on a table in the parlor. Honor had borrowed it and was reading it with deep interest, but she ought to have kept it out of sight.

Playing for time, she said, "This letter is a perfect disgrace."

"There's nothing in it that isn't true. You can't stop me sending it."

"Oh yes, I can." A way was now clear to her. "I am not talking about your opinions, Nancy. I am talking about your writing and spelling. They are both quite shocking. I should not dream of allowing such a sample to go out from here. It would do the school far more harm than your rather silly remarks. I wouldn't have thought it possible that anyone could make eleven spelling mistakes in six lines, but you have managed it. When you have corrected every mistake and made a fair copy without any blots, you may send it to your parents, but not before."

She felt this was a safe risk to take.

"How am I know which of the words are wrong?"

"You must find out for yourself. I suppose you can use a dictionary?"

Nancy looked baffled, and less confident than usual. "Didn't Corisande or Sally make any mistakes? You passed their letters."

"They didn't make any blots," said Honor firmly. "They are both younger than you, but they don't write like babies."

This was a partial victory, but it was pitiful to feel proud of winning a contest of wits against a child of thirteen.

"I don't know what we are to do with her," Honor confessed to Lucy that evening. "She seems to be quite beyond ordinary rules and sanctions."

"And she is having a bad effect on the others. Do you think we should write and tell her parents we are unable to keep her? We should be in good company, after all."

"I don't think we can. Not just at present. I have been looking up Mrs. Newlander's letter. We were recommended to her by old Miss Barnes, who was a distant connection of my mother's, and who lives near Exeter and knows everyone for miles around. She is one of the few people who is really trying to get us pupils, and I think she may very well send us more. But if Nancy goes home and announces that we are disciples of Mary Wollstonecraft, the fat will be properly in the fire and not another little darling will we get."

Mary Wollstonecraft's illegitimate child and her marriage to an atheist had condemned *The Rights of Women*, unread, in the minds of the respectable.

"Though there is nothing in her book that anyone could object to," said Lucy. "Surely it must be true that educated women make better wives and mothers? That's all she claims for them."

"Educated women are a threat to stupid women. And a menace to stupid men. How difficult everything is! And the Marlows, going off and leaving their children without a friend in the world except you and me. I expect all schools have awkward pupils and parents, but surely we have an undue share?"

Lucy was darning a stocking in the lamplight. She looked up.

"Doesn't it strike you that a lot of people have taken advantage of our inexperience?"

Honor thought this over. "Yes, I am afraid you are right. There doesn't seem to be much wrong with Corisande."

"She is a terrible little storyteller; she told the other girls her father was a duke. Margaret asked me if it was true. However, that isn't very serious," added Lucy, smiling. "Lots of children make up fairytales about themselves."

"Then we need not lose any sleep over that. And I don't think Sally will give us any trouble."

(2)

In spite of its troubles, the school soon got into its stride. This was largely due to Lucy, who was an inspired teacher. She made their lessons so interesting that everyone except Nancy wanted to learn, and even Nancy lost a little of her arrogance and bluster when she realized that no one would listen to her when they could hear Miss Fielder talking about Greek myths or Mary, Queen of Scots or the discoveries of Captain Cook. Honor taught music to the younger girls and took the needlework classes. She also taught French and drawing for the time being, which cut down on the expense of visiting masters.

They had engaged an Italian lady to teach extra music and singing; she was to come in twice a week, and there was a dapper little man who arrived every Monday to give a dancing lesson, his miniature fiddle tucked under his chin. Otherwise they could manage on their own.

Honor had charge of the housekeeping, which she enjoyed until it began to dawn on her that there was not quite enough money to go round. She was puzzled; she had done her sums so carefully beforehand, and if they had fewer pupils than they had originally hoped for, that must mean that they bought less food. Of course it wasn't only the pupils who had to be fed. She and Lucy and the four servants, as well as the boarders, had to be maintained on the fees. The cost of what they ate would easily be absorbed in a household of twenty-five. With the present number it was impossible. Yet she couldn't reduce the servants; that would at once sink the school into a much more rough-and-ready category, not the exclusive seminary for young ladies which Mrs. Bilting and Miss Butley, for instance, were paying for. She would have to squeeze the extra house-

41

keeping money out of her private resources, let her unpaid bills run a little longer, and hope that none of the tradesmen would start dunning her.

How tiresome it was, having to pinch and scrape, she thought, as she set out one afternoon to look for a shop that was reputed to sell the cheapest candles. As she approached the front door, she heard someone outside come up the steps. Who could this be? She peeped through the little circular window beside the door. The person on the step chose the same moment to look in, and she found herself confronted by the swarthy, staring face of a man, so close to her own that but for the pane of glass they might have been kissing. Embarrassed, she drew back her head and opened the door.

The visitor was a stocky individual, perhaps a foreigner, for besides his dark complexion and rather wild black locks, he was very oddly dressed in a lurid violet coat with a dandified, pinched-in waist, heavy frogging and glossy buttons. His breeches bagged at the knee and his boots were too pointed.

"I wish to see the lady who keeps the school."

The voice was perfectly English. Who and what could he be? Surely not an inquiring parent? She was immediately on her guard, for this vulgar-looking person was not the sort they wanted to encourage.

"I am Miss Clare," she said coolly. "Perhaps, if you have any business with me, you would write and make an appointment, Mr. . . . ?"

"Colvin. If you are going out, I will come in and wait. I should like in the meantime to see my daughter."

"I think you have made a mistake, sir. Your

42

daughter is not—good heavens, did you say Colvin?"

"I see you know the name," said the stranger, calmly entering the house and shutting the door behind him.

"We have a Miss Colvin, but she is an orphan!"

"Did my good sister-in-law tell you that? Or did she just imply that she was Sally's nearest relative, and leave you to make the assumption? She's inclined to do so when it suits her."

Honor tried to remember exactly what Miss Butley had said about her niece. She took Mr. Colvin into the parlor and then walked through into the schoolroom at the back. It was the regular playtime and most of the girls were out in the garden. Skipping was their great craze: four little figures in colored gingham hopped and bobbed as the ropes swung over their heads and under their feet in loops and circles. Corisande and the three Marlows were happily chanting *Oranges and Lemons* as they skipped.

Honor called out of the window. "Martha, will you go and find Sally for me, if you please? Ask her to come to the parlor."

"Yes, Miss Clare."

Honor returned to Mr. Colvin. She found him standing in the middle of the small room, staring suspiciously about him.

"Sally will be here in a moment," she said. "Won't you be seated?"

He took a chair and leaned back, crossing his legs. She noticed that his eyes were unusually light for such a dark skinned man. She tried to make polite conversation, but he did not respond.

Time passed. Mr. Colvin consulted his watch

and drummed his fingers on the arm of the chair. What on earth could Martha be doing?

"I'd better go and find her myself," said Honor.

Mr. Colvin gave her a sharp glance.

"If this delay is a device to prevent me from seeing my daughter I had better warn you, ma'am, not to be foolhardy. No matter what inducements the Butleys may have held out."

She was too astonished to answer.

The door opened and Lucy peeped in, looking agitated. "Can I speak to you for a moment?"

Honor went out into the passage. "What is it? I can't come now, I've got this extraordinary man who says he's Sally's father—"

"Oh dear, is that why you wanted her? How very unlucky. We've been searching high and low, she's nowhere in the house or garden."

"But she can't have vanished!"

"Nancy is missing too. I'm afraid they have slipped out into the town without permission."

"Good God!" exclaimed Honor, in dismay.

Martha was also in the passage. She said, "I think I know where they've gone, Miss Clare. Nancy tried to persuade Margaret to go with her to see the Cabinet of Gems. Just for a lark, only I told Meg it was wrong and anyway she couldn't pay to go in. But Sally was there too, and she has plenty of pocket money."

"Well, thank goodness we know that much." Honor came to a swift decision. She was already dressed for the street. "I'll go and bring them back, it won't take long. Lucy, you must pacify Mr. Colvin. Tell him his daughter has gone to a music lesson—anything you please."

She was out of the house before Lucy had time to object, and racing down Belmont as fast as she could go in a tight skirt and with very little of the dignity due from the principal of a select boarding school.

The Cabinet of Gems on Union Street was a collection of rare and beautiful objects which she and Lucy had visited soon after coming to Bath; they had promised to take the girls there one day as a treat. Nancy had sneered at the prospect—and then gone off there on her own. Just what one might expect, only why did she have to tempt good little Sally to join her, and on this particular day? It was most unfortunate.

Honor skimmed through the broad stream of traffic, in danger of her life, and was just entering Milsom Street when Mr. Colvin overtook her.

"Where exactly is my daughter?"

"I am going to fetch her. It had slipped my memory that she had gone to visit an exhibition in the City. With an older companion. There was no need for you to follow me, sir. I did leave a message."

"Some frightened-looking female tried to stop me as I left the house."

"That lady was my partner, Miss Fielder," Honor said stiffly.

"Then she has good reason to be frightened," snapped Mr. Colvin.

They were hurrying down Milsom Street and receiving a good many curious stares from the fashionable strollers. She caught a glimpse of herself and her unwelcome escort reflected in a shop window, and a very odd couple they made: she in her deep mourning and the ill-mannered person in the flashy coat. His cheap smartness was not in keeping with his grim expression.

Thank God they were in Union Street at last.

She turned into the Cabinet of Gems and asked whether the two young ladies were still there.

"It's very educational," she added, for the benefit of Mr. Colvin.

He slapped down some coins and marched in ahead of her.

The mainstay of the exhibition was a display of tiny statuettes, carved in onyx and not more than two inches high, mostly copied from the figures on the Etruscan vases in Sir William Hamilton's famous collection. There were other items too, and they found the truants gazing at the most spectacular: a mechanical singing bird, which spread its silver wings, opened its beak and trilled the song of the nightingale in notes of precise, delicious sweetness from a musical box in its throat. The two girls were entranced. For the first time Honor saw Nancy looking pleased and interested like an ordinary child. Then Sally glanced round and gave a squeak of guilt and fright. Nancy turned and her expression became clouded with its usual sulky defiance.

"I suppose that sniveling Martha told you where to find us," she remarked. "What a spoilsport she is."

Mr. Colvin was watching Sally. "Do you know who I am?"

"No," said Sally, not attending. Her eyes were fixed on Miss Clare, the dreaded bringer of retribution.

"Well! You've changed more than I have in three years, but I should have known you anywhere. Look at me, Sally."

This did make her notice him and her face grew very pink.

"Is it—you cannot be—are you my Papa?"

46

"Yes, I'm your Papa."

He bent to touch her shoulder. Honor thought he was going to kiss her, but he didn't. Sally, her nerves overstretched, burst into tears.

No one had much to say as the strange little party trailed back up the hill to Belmont. Mr. Colvin held his daughter's hand. Honor gripped Nancy's arm.

When they reached the school, Honor showed the Colvins into the best of the upstairs rooms. It was elegantly furnished, for she had imagined their talented pupils giving concerts there, or performing plays, in front of their admiring relations. So far it had never been used. She left the father and daughter together.

Nancy had gone upstairs on her own initiative. With the numbers still so low, she had been given a front room to herself on the second floor. She had kicked her shoes off and was sitting on the bed, munching an almond cake. (The expedition must have made a foraging sortie on the way to the Cabinet of Gems.)

Honor said, "You have behaved extremely badly, Nancy, not only in leaving the house yourself but in persuading Sally to go with you. You will be locked in your room for the rest of the evening."

As she turned the key, she half expected a rude and noisy outburst, but none came. That was a relief, at any rate. She went downstairs. Her head was aching after so much running about in anxiety. Lucy had the rest of the girls in the schoolroom; it was an arithmetic lesson and they were reciting their tables. Honor sat in the parlor with the door open, waiting for Mr. Colvin to come down.

At last he and Sally emerged from the upper floor, looking rather easier in each other's company.

"I'm sorry to leave you, pet," he was saying. "But I have things I must do. I shall come again in the morning. Now run away and join your friends. I want to talk to Miss Clare."

Sally lifted up her face and this time he kissed her. Then she scampered off quite happily. Her father's presence had apparently wiped out the memory of her crime. It was Honor who felt like a criminal, dealing for the first time with a dissatisfied parent who had some reason to complain.

"I'm sorry Sally was not here when you arrived," she said, hoping to placate him. "I'm afraid the whole episode was a trifle unorthodox, but it has never happened before, and won't again, I assure you."

"It certainly won't happen to Sally. I shall be removing her from this school as soon as I have made other arrangements."

Honor had been dreading this.

"Please don't come to a hasty decision." She was obliged to plead, while despising herself for the necessity. "She is happy here, and you must admit that she came to no harm—"

"Small thanks to you, ma'am. A nine-year-old girl to be running about the city like a vagabond! And with such a companion! Well, I have my own opinion about what is liable to harm my daughter. I shall have to leave her with you for the time being, but I hope you will be ready to pack her clothes at short notice."

Honor was wondering unhappily whether to make a further appeal when she noticed that several people had stopped on the pavement outside

48

the house and were staring upwards. Then Pinker the parlormaid came bursting in.

"Oh, if you please, miss! There's a man come to the basement door says there's something wrong! One of the young ladies—"

Mr. Colvin, having had his say, was preparing to leave without any more discussion. As he opened the front door, they could hear someone shouting, high above the street. Honor followed him out.

It was, predictably, Nancy making a scene. She had thrown up her sash window to its full extent and was leaning out, her hair wild, her shoulders bare, proclaiming her wrongs in a high, unearthly moan.

"Save me! Save me! . . . kept a prisoner . . . chained up and starved!"

I'll kill her for this, thought Honor. She herself was now becoming the focus of pointing fingers and angry murmurs, though a rather beery carter said loudly that this was as good as a play. He was pretty near the mark, especially when Nancy cried, "Help me, good people!" in the manner of a persecuted queen about to be rescued by her loyal subjects.

"What are you proposing to do about that?" inquired Mr. Colvin, disagreeably. "Haven't you even a semblance of authority over your pupils? I shall be thankful to get Sally out of this madhouse!"

He strode off down the Lansdown Road without waiting for an answer.

Lucy and several of the girls had now ventured out, but retreated on seeing the hostile crowd. Honor went with them. What are we to do? she wondered desperately.

Of course they must go and drag Nancy away from the window, but unless they really did treat her like a prisoner, she would go on making life intolerable. She had already lost them one of their best pupils, and when Mr. Colvin said the place was like a madhouse, one was forced to agree.

This gave her an idea.

She turned to Lucy. "I want you to come upstairs with me and agree to everything I say."

"I generally do."

"Yes, but this time you must pretend, whether you agree or not."

As they reached the second floor, they could hear Nancy still shouting. There was a small table on the landing, with a brass jug on it. Honor gave it a push, as though by accident, to attract Nancy's attention. As she expected, the shouting stopped. Nancy was listening, preparing no doubt for the next encounter.

In a clear, conversational voice, Honor said to Lucy, "It is tiresome that Dr. Strang has been delayed. I sent for him as soon as we got back from Union Street. Now I am not sure whether to order the carriage for tonight or tomorrow morning..."

"The carriage?" repeated Lucy, uncertain of her lines.

"To take her to Bristol, my dear. You know the asylum is in Bristol."

Lucy, looking completely horrified, was about to say so but Honor gave her a warning nudge, and she was silent.

"I am told it is a most humane asylum," added Honor.

"Oh yes. That is to say—I suppose such a dreadful solution—"

"Is quite unavoidable. That is what Dr. Strang

said himself when I discussed the matter with him last week. 'If Miss Newlander becomes any more erratic,' he said, 'she will have to be put away.'"

All this was sheer nonsense; she had not sent for the doctor, she had never consulted him about Nancy, though he had come to the school last week when Corisande had a sore throat. A board creaked in the room opposite. Lucy was still looking horrified. Honor made a pantomime face at her, pointed towards the stairs, and then unlocked Nancy's door.

Nancy had left the window and was over by the bed.

"I'm not mad," she said.

"Of course not, my dear child," said Honor in a bright, soothing voice.

She was pleased to see that this shook Nancy a good deal, for she was so clearly speaking as a kind person humoring a lunatic, not as an angry teacher with a rebellious pupil.

"You have not been yourself, lately," she continued, "and you will be more comfortable in a hospital where they can take good care of you."

"There's nothing wrong with me. You can't send me to Bedlam."

Honor went across to shut the window and saw with satisfaction that the crowd in the street had begun to disperse.

Nancy had taken off her dress and pulled her hair over her face to make her performance more convincing. This really did give her a slightly demented look. She seemed conscious of this and scrambled into her dress again.

She said, with a trace of uncertainty, "You can't get me shut up."

"Only for your own good."

51

"If you try to say I'm mad, no one will believe you."

"Don't you think so? A girl who announces to the whole of Bath that she is starving, when everyone in the house can testify how much she has eaten today?"

"But that's different! I just said that because—"

"Because you have a spiteful nature and you want to stir up as much trouble as possible. Yes, I am aware. But I shall never say such a thing outside this room. I shall simply say that you have been suffering from delusions. It is a far more charitable explanation."

The two adversaries stared at each other and Honor knew she had won. She had taken Nancy's measure and almost accidentally found the way to deal with her. For several years Nancy had been able to establish a reign of terror over those around her, because they knew how outrageously she could behave if she was thwarted. Sulks, obstinacy, rudeness, physical resistance, humiliating public scenes—she didn't mind using any of these weapons, she rather enjoyed them, in fact. But her opponents minded very much. In particular they shrank from the public scenes. As a result they gave in far too easily, anything for a quiet life.

But Nancy could only succeed as long as she went unchallenged. If two equally unscrupulous egotists met in a head-on collision, victory was bound to go to the older and more experienced, the one who started from a position of advantage.

Nancy was quite intelligent enough to realize this, and she was plainly wondering whether Miss Clare was wicked and daring enough to put her

in a madhouse. If she had been a very little bit
older, she must have been able to calculate how
unlikely this was. But in spite of her power to
cause havoc and her independent character, she
was still a child, living in a world of melodrama
and exaggeration. She had gone too far and now
she had lost her nerve.

"You have the remedy in your own hands,"
Honor told her. "If you want to be treated as a
rational being, you must behave like one."

(3)

"I am surprised at her believing you," said Lucy.
"Luckily she does."

"If she is now prepared to behave more reasonably, it will be better for us all. But what a sad
picture of life she must have, to suppose that you
seriously intended anything so wicked."

Honor felt a qualm of pity for Nancy. They simply could not have her carrying on in such an
undisciplined way, yet once she and Sally had
found themselves at liberty in the streets of Bath,
their trip to the Cabinet of Gems had been curiously innocent and would have done no real harm,
but for the arrival of Mr. Colvin.

"Why could not Sally's father have warned us
he was coming? And what is she doing with such
a man for a father? So thoroughly second-rate.
And I don't trust him. His eyes are far too close
together."

"I didn't see much of him," said Lucy. "I thought
he sounded to have the voice of a gentleman."

"A passable imitation, at least." Honor considered this. "His voice was the best thing about him,
but his clothes and his manners were atrocious,

though in different ways, which seems odd. I should have expected the man who wore that coat to smile too much and be overfamiliar. Instead, he was churlish and rude."

"You are forgetting your altered station." Lucy spoke with the occasional dryness that always took Honor by surprise. "Men such as you describe don't waste their ingratiating smiles on their inferiors: tradesmen or servants or the teachers in a school."

So all the time that she had been despising Mr. Colvin, probably Mr. Colvin had been despising her. Honor could not help seeing the comic side of this, though she was not in the mood to be amused for long.

"He will take Sally away, which is bad enough; I shall be very sorry to lose her. Then he will give a critical account of us to the Butleys and they will tell the Robinsons, where your sister is, and we shall get no new girls from that quarter. I was beginning to have high hopes of that set of people, they sound so rich and reliable. Lucy, what are we to do?"

Lucy sipped her tea. Their evening tea drinking had become the pleasantest hour of the day, when they could talk without interruption and enjoy the harmony and companionship of two people who got on well together. It was at these times Honor felt most thankful that she had escaped from Sidney and Euphemia. She liked to have the tray set on her mother's pembroke table, the silver spirit-kettle faintly hissing, and the Coalport service with its wide band of dark blue and gold and the painted roses. Though there was not much pleasure to be had this evening.

"What are we to do?" she repeated.

"I don't think we ought to let Mr. Colvin take Sally away," said Lucy, after some thought.

Honor was astounded. Lucy was generally so timid and law-abiding; life had made her so.

"Not let him take her! How can we prevent him? Surely you aren't turning into what Nancy calls a Revlushonary?"

"I have been thinking it over, and it all seems so strange. Sally hasn't talked of her father as the other girls do, and I gather she didn't even recognize him to start with."

"No, she didn't. Good heavens, are you suggesting that he isn't her father after all? That he's trying to abduct her? To obtain a large ransom?"

"You've been reading too many Gothic novels! I think he must be her father, but we don't know whether he has the right to take her away. It was Miss Butley who left her in our care."

"Surely there can be no question? Fathers have every legal right where their children are concerned, and mothers have none: that's what you might call one of the principal Wrongs of Women. And Miss Butley isn't even Sally's mother, just an aunt."

"All the same, I can't help wondering.... The Robinsons seem to have accepted Mrs. Colvin as a widow. The Butleys, as you say, are very rich. If Mr. Colvin is what you call thoroughly second-rate, she may have made an imprudent marriage, against the wishes of her family."

"I should think it very likely."

"When that happens," said Lucy, "the husband is sometimes bought off later on. Given so many thousand pounds to go away and leave his wife in peace; of course they make him sign a great many documents renouncing his claims before he gets the money. I heard of such a case when I was in my first place; my employer's sister had been very foolish and had to be rescued from the most miserable situation. The children were made wards in chancery."

"If Sally is a ward in chancery, Miss Butley ought to have told us so."

"Mr. Rose ought to have told us that Evelina had fits. I may be absolutely wrong, only I cannot help thinking that if Sally's parents had separated, there must have been some kind of agreement about who was to have charge of her, and we are bound to refer to Miss Butley."

"Yes, I am sure that would be wise. We'll write to her tomorrow."

Honor's first preoccupation in the morning was Nancy; she had been feeling rather guilty about their last encounter. It would be dreadful if the wretched girl really came to believe she was going mad and might be locked up in the nearest asylum. She was soon reassured. Though sulky and silent, Nancy was not in the least cowed, she looked as though she had slept properly (you could always tell with anyone so young) and she had a good breakfast with second helpings of everything. Clearly she knew she was in no danger of the madhouse or any other unpleasant fate so long as she behaved herself.

So Honor could concentrate on thinking out the letter that must be written to Miss Butley, and hoping they would get a reply before Sally's father tried to take her away.

It was a vain hope. An hour later Honor was called out of a French lesson to deal with Mr. Colvin. He had driven up in a post chaise with a respectable maidservant whom he had engaged to look after Sally, and who was going to pack her clothes.

"How soon can she be ready?" he asked in a peremptory manner. "I don't want to keep the horses waiting."

He was looking slightly more presentable today, with a freshly starched neckcloth and a pair of fawn trousers which were an improvement on those pointed boots. The flashy coat was as contemptible as ever, and it gave her the courage to stand up to him.

"Miss Fielder and I have been considering, Mr. Colvin, and we both feel that we cannot allow you to take Sally away until we have consulted Miss Butley."

"What the devil has it to do with Miss Butley? I'm the child's father."

He had flushed with annoyance, which deepened the color of his skin, and the light, angry eyes in the dark face made her think suddenly of a cat. Not a sleek old tabby either, but a fierce and dangerous predator.

"If you will just listen for one moment—"

"I suppose you will be saying next that I'm not her father!"

As Honor had said this already, it was quite a struggle not to tell him so.

"Miss Butley placed Sally in our charge and paid her fees, so it seems to us we are responsible to her."

"Is it your idea of responsibility to let Sally run wild in the streets of Bath whenever the fancy takes her?"

"That is an absurd exaggeration. She has never done so before—"

"The other child has, apparently. She boasted to Sally that she goes out as often as she chooses."

She would, thought Honor bitterly. There was no end to the trouble Nancy could make for them, even without trying.

"I think Sally has been taken in. Miss Newlander will tell tall stories to anyone who is willing to listen."

"Oh? So she is a hardened liar? I suppose that renders her a most suitable example for a little girl of nine? Heaven preserve me from the logic of a bluestocking!"

Honor was beginning to say furiously that she was not a bluestocking, when she realized in time that this would be a denial of her new status as an independent woman, the mistress of her own school.

Instead she said, "I see how it is. You are against female education, like most of your sex."

"I am against any education which unfits a woman for the demands of ordinary life. Such as taking proper care of a child who has been entrusted to her charge."

"Very well, Mr. Colvin. Your sister-in-law entrusted Sally to me and I shall not let her go. If you attempt to remove her from this school I shall inform a magistrate."

He stared at her, apparently incredulous. She was too angry to be frightened by his murderous expression. Lucy, who had just joined them, glanced from one to the other in genuine alarm.

"Can't we come to a peaceful solution?" she said in her gentle voice. "Mr. Colvin, I'm sure you can appreciate how awkwardly we are placed. Sally's aunt brought her here and asked us to undertake her education. All we need is a letter from her,

58

confirming that this contract is now at an end. Of course we are sorry that you are not satisfied with the school, but this is not why we are trying to make difficulties. We simply need you to indemnify us against any complaint from Miss Butley. You may act without her permission but we cannot do so."

"Very correct," said Colvin, scowling.

He made no further attempt to abduct his daughter, merely asking to see her for a few minutes before he set out for London alone. Honor and Lucy were thankful to see him go.

Mr. Colvin had several things to see to before actually leaving Bath. He paid off the maid, handsomely enough to make up for her disappointment, and then returned to the York Hotel, where he had spent the night. Having asked for a gazetteer which dealt with the county of Sussex, he looked up the villages of Brauncing and Storham, calculated the distance between them, and sat down to write a letter.

PART THREE

Parents and Guardians

"No, Dick—you must not!" said Henrietta Delahaye, standing perfectly still in the middle of the Brauncing parsonage drawing room. Her laughing, breathless voice clearly meant, "do go on."

Richard Lyman went on kissing the back of her neck and then turned her gently so that he could kiss her mouth for the first time. He was twenty-one, a slim young man with a charming smile and a touch of arrogance in his manner that girls found attractive. He had been playing this game very skillfully for several years. Henrietta had never played it before. She was fifteen, pretty and affectionate, needing love and wanting excitement.

"How sweet you are," he murmured. "Dear little Hen."

They were enjoying themselves so much that they did not hear the door open, and the Reverend John Porcheston caught them in each other's arms.

"Richard! Henrietta!"

They jumped apart so guiltily that Henrietta almost fell against the sofa table and Mrs. Porcheston's Chelsea shepherd and shepherdess trembled and slithered on the polished wood.

Dick retained enough self-possession to say, "Henrietta had an eyelash in her eye sir, and I was helping her get it out. Has it gone, now, Henrietta?"

"Oh. Yes. Yes, thank you."

Henrietta's eyelashes fluttered wildly. They were very long and dark. She had violet blue eyes and dark red hair that would never be called ginger. She looked nervously at Mr. Porcheston.

"Go to your room, miss," he commanded. "At once!"

"Yes, sir," whispered Henrietta, and fled.

Left alone to face the angry clergyman, Dick became glib.

"I know it must have looked bad, sir—I assure you it wasn't at all what you thought. Henrietta is such a child, she thinks of me as a brother..."

"She is a child, and you are not her brother. Which makes the whole situation peculiarly disgraceful. You come here and abuse our hospitality by playing on the artless affection of a girl who is still in the schoolroom, a motherless girl who has been placed in our care. You will leave this house today and you will not return, so long as Henrietta is living with us. Do you understand me?"

Dick understood him only too well. He was beginning to beg for a reprieve, with all sorts of promises of good behavior, while calculating how much money he had in the world, when Mrs. Porcheston came in from the hall.

"Whatever is the matter, John? I could hear you shouting when I was in the garden."

"Come here, Cecilia, and close the door. I have just caught Dick making love to Henrietta."

Mrs. Porcheston gazed reproachfully at her godson.

"Dick, you wretch! How could you be so naughty?"

"I'm very sorry, Cousin Cecilia. I didn't mean it to happen."

"Naughty!" repeated John Porcheston. "Is that what you call it? Well, I take a more serious view, and I have told Dick he can pack and leave. After this I won't run the risk of having him and Henrietta in the same house."

"Oh, but that is too severe!" cried his wife, now really distressed. "And quite unnecessary, I'm sure Dick won't be so thoughtless again." She glanced at her white-faced protégé. "Dick, would you go into the garden and see what William is up to? I left him there alone and he's probably pulling the heads off the tulips by now."

She had got rid of Dick rather neatly, she thought, as he left her to fight his battles.

"In your eyes, I suppose," said her husband, "Dick's kissing Henrietta and William's pulling up the tulips are sins of about equal gravity?"

He was a handsome man, standing in the long, white drawing room of the Sussex rectory. Sometimes he seemed a little too heavy on his feet and deliberate, but anger gave a keen edge to both his profile and his manner, and she knew that this was one of the times when she would have to go carefully.

"Of course it was reckless and imprudent of Dick," she said. "Of Henrietta too, for I expect she was equally to blame. I am sure he did not mean to do anything wrong."

"My dear girl, what he was doing *was* wrong,

whether he meant it or not. It can never be right to awaken the passions of a child of fifteen. I don't suggest that Dick would try to seduce her, I hope he's not such a scoundrel. Merely to flirt with such a very young girl might raise false hopes and cause her a great deal of misery and heartbreak. And the remaining possibility, a serious attachment, is something we cannot even contemplate. General Delahaye pays us to look after his orphaned granddaughter, he trusts us to give her a good home and to protect her from the mistakes of youth and inexperience. He would not wish her to fall in love and become engaged at fifteen; even if it was a most brilliant match, I'm sure he would consider her too young. And as for letting her throw herself away on a penniless nobody, he would never give his consent. You must remember that Henrietta is a great heiress."

"I do remember," retorted his wife. "It was the first thing I thought of when I saw how much she and Dick liked each other."

For a moment he was too stupefied to speak. Then he said, in what she called his homily-reading voice, "If you mean that seriously, I am ashamed of you! Are you suggesting that we should encourage her to fall in love with your godson while they are thrown together in our house and she is too innocent to realize that he is after her money? I call that downright wicked."

Cecilia's white skin turned a vivid pink. She had always blushed easily, much to her annoyance. She was a tall, fair woman; at thirty-four and the mother of five children, she had kept her looks, her natural optimism and her appetite for the good things of life.

"He would not be simply after her money," she

63

insisted. "They like each other exceedingly, that is the whole point. Henrietta is bound to marry someone, so why shouldn't it be Dick? A fine young man, talented and charming, with every gift that is needed to make a girl happy. It is true he has no fortune, but hers is a large one, so what does it matter?"

"You really are quite besotted about that boy," said her husband in disgust. "Leaving aside the moral issue, can you not see how fatal it would be for us if Henrietta was to fall in love with Dick while she was living in this house? General Delahaye would be furious and he would naturally complain to Midhurst, who would turn us out of the parsonage, out of the parish, and would certainly never raise a finger to help me again. I should find myself without a living and without a patron. And don't imagine, as I'm sure you must have been imagining, that once Henrietta married Dick we could turn to them for support and advancement. The General is a recluse but he may easily live another fifteen or twenty years. If he did, he might forgive Henrietta, he might even come to accept Dick, but I feel certain he would never forgive us. So we should be left high and dry, having lost Lord Midhurst's good opinion long before we could hope for anything from this hole-and-corner marriage you are eager to promote."

Cecilia did not reply. She was shrewd enough to know he was talking sense. Eight years ago, when they married, neither of them had much money, but she had been convinced that John would become a bishop in no time at all, or at least receive some valuable preferment. He was such an excellent clergyman, so good looking, so impressive in the church, his sermons were so well delivered, while he and she were both so well connected. Unluckily their connections were not quite strong enough. All their friends seemed to have at least five relations who were parsons and John was not at the top of anyone's list. They had eventually been befriended by the Earl of Midhurst, patron of the very rich living of Brauncing which he wanted kept warm for one of his nephews, a boy who was still at school. If John Porcheston would minister to the faithful in Brauncing for the next few years, until young Charles was ready to be ordained, his lordship would be uncommonly grateful. It was tacitly understood that he would then do something else for John as a reward. The Earl was a generous man, aware of their large family and limited means, and it was he who had suggested to old General Delahaye that they might be the right people to bring up and educate his granddaughter Henrietta, who had lost both her parents in tragic circumstances.

The Porchestons had been living very comfortably at Brauncing for the last five years and it was sometimes hard to remember that John was not really the rector. If he had been, they would have been safe, for he could not then have been cast out of this Eden for anything less than flagrant immorality or heresy, two sins he was not at all likely to commit. As things were, they could not afford to get on the wrong side of Midhurst, who could turn them out at a moment's notice.

Cecilia looked around her pretty drawing room and out of the window at the velvet lawn and the beech tree, the shrubbery where plumes of lilac were breaking into flower. Beyond, she could see the distant roll of the Downs. They could not lose all this. She saw Dick crossing the grass, leading by the hand Master William Porcheston, aged four, the potential destroyer of tulips, and she felt a stab of resentment, not against Dick but against Henrietta. It was all her fault that they had been found out, silly little minx.

A servant came in, soft footed, bringing a letter on a silver salver.

"From Storham, madam. The man is waiting for a reply."

Cecilia read the letter.

"How odd," she said to John, anxious to distract him, for he was still looking solemn. "Mrs. Weldon writes that they are coming over tomorrow to look at the Abbey. They have a friend staying, a Mr. Colvin, who is interested in ruins, and may they call on me afterwards? Well, of course they may, but why did she write to ask? What is it they want?"

"I expect they want me to show them round the ruins. People generally do."

"Yes, but if that was all, why didn't Colonel Weldon write to you direct? Do you think they are hinting for us to ask them to dinner?"

She was rather put out, for it was short notice, and the Weldons were rich people who lived in a style she could only emulate if she had plenty of time to prepare. There ought to be two full courses and several other guests, and all the silver polished and on the table. It was so awkward to be rushed. She hardly knew the Weldons and could not bear to entertain them in a way that would make them look down on her.

"I don't think they want to dine with us," said John, when he had read the note. "They are coming in the morning, much too early for dinner. I tell you what I think: Mrs. Weldon would like to come in here after they have been walking about the Abbey, to have a short rest and perhaps a cool drink before going home. After all, it is a twelve mile drive. She has written to make sure it will be convenient."

"You are probably right," agreed Cecilia, brightening, for this kind of informal visit presented no difficulties.

She wrote a graceful little note to Mrs. Weldon, and then returned in her mind to the problem of Dick and Henrietta. Poor Dick, it was too bad that he was the one who had to be sent away. She was so very fond of him, though it was unkind of John to use the word besotted. His mother had been a family friend, an older girl she had greatly admired; when Mary married and had asked her to be godmother to her baby, the young Cecilia Phillips had been immensely happy and proud. For the next thirteen years, until her own marriage, he had been the child who mattered to her more than any other, and after his mother's death and his father's second marriage, she had done her best to fill Mary's place.

She went upstairs to scold Henrietta.

(2)

"We are nearly at Brauncing," said Mrs. Weldon, as the carriage swung cautiously off the turnpike road and past some weathered cottages. "Do you want us to mention the real reason for your visit?"

"I think not," said Marcus Colvin, "I should prefer to make up my mind about the Porchestons first."

Since leaving Bath, he had been to London,

quarreled with his dead wife's sister and visited his tailor. He was now quietly and suitably dressed for a morning call in the country, his brown coat and light pantaloons extremely well cut but in no way exaggerated.

He was looking for somewhere to send Sally once he got her away from that abominable school, and having heard recently that Mr. & Mrs. Porcheston had taken one motherless girl into their family, he thought they might accept another. His friends the Weldons lived in the same corner of Sussex, so he had enlisted their help.

"The parson is a good fellow," Colonel Weldon was saying. "And very well liked. Better than his wife, perhaps."

"She gives herself airs," Mrs. Weldon amplified. "Which is so stupid and quite unnecessary. They say she is only interested in people she can make use of. But I don't want to put you off."

"Thank you," said Colvin. "You have already done so."

It had been agreed that they should meet Mr. Porcheston at the Abbey. They were a little early and Colonel Weldon told his coachman to take the carriage round to the Parsonage stables. They got out onto the gravel sweep, not intending to enter the house, but Mr. Porcheston saw them from a window and asked them in.

"My wife is coming with us," he said, meeting them on the doorstep. "She will not keep you waiting above a moment."

The hall was large and airy, with a high screen of Italian gilded leather across one corner, probably to keep out some of the draughts. On the other side of this screen, a woman was speaking in a clear, hard voice.

"He has gone now, so there's nothing to be done about it. For heaven's sake stop wailing, Henrietta. And try not to make a fool of yourself in front of the visitors."

"I can't stop...I can't meet anyone...you are so unkind!"

A young girl in a white dress almost flew across the hall, her hair in a tangle, the tears streaming down her face. She ran sobbing up the stairs as Mrs. Porcheston followed her round the corner of the screen and saw her visitors.

There was a hiatus of wordless awkwardness, then she recovered sufficiently to come forward, saying, "My dear Mrs. Weldon, do please forgive us—we have been having a little storm in a teacup and you came in for the last act."

Marcus Colvin was forced to admire her poise, though he had instantly decided that he would not wish to put Sally in her care. He did not know what the weeping Henrietta had done; she had probably been very tiresome, girls often were. He knew that he did not like the cold contempt in Mrs. Porcheston's voice, and that was enough. Now he would have to endure the tedium of being shown round this confounded ruin, and all to no purpose.

Studiously making conversation, they walked along a shady road lined with chestnut trees and came in sight of Brauncing Abbey. Unlike so many old religious buildings, it had never been transformed into a secular mansion. The Earl of Midhurst lived on one of his other estates, and there had never been a great house at Brauncing; the abbey had decayed to a shell, for which most people blamed Cromwell (Thomas or Oliver, according to choice). It was really due to the local inhabitants, who had started by stripping the lead off the roof and had gone on removing stones for their own uses, during the past three centuries.

The skeleton church looked graceful rather than gaunt against the green of the Downs and the blue May sky: a pattern of tall pillars and fretted arches and the vacant circle that had once held a rose window.

Mr. Porcheston now began to describe the lost glories of Brauncing and the life of the medieval monks. Marcus Colvin did his best to look attentive, though the twelfth century bored him. Rather to his relief, his name had conveyed nothing to the parson, whose interests seemed to be parochial in every sense of the word. After they had been round the church, they had to tour the stunted walls and overgrown foundations of the monastery, trying to identify the dormitories, cloisters and refectory. At last the treat was over and they turned back towards the parsonage.

Colvin now found himself walking beside Mrs. Porcheston. She was still acutely embarrassed because they had overheard part of her scene with Henrietta, and she wanted to justify herself.

"I don't know what you must be thinking of us, Mr. Colvin. Such an unfortunate display just as you were arriving! I'm afraid poor little Henrietta has no command over her feelings, girls of her age are apt to make mountains out of molehills."

"So I have been told. Is Miss Henrietta your niece? I am sure she cannot be your daughter."

He knew perfectly well who Henrietta was, but did not wish to say so. The question pleased and flattered Cecilia, who could easily have been Henrietta's mother; there were nineteen years between them. She smiled approvingly at Mr. Col-

70

vin. A fine-looking man she thought him, impeccably dressed, and his tailor knew how to show off his broad, muscular shoulders to advantage.

"Henrietta Delahaye is no relation, of course," she said. "The Delahayes are a very old family, as I dare say you know, with property in the Scilly Isles, and she is her grandfather's sole surviving heir. There was a shocking tragedy three years ago, when her parents and grandparents were crossing to the mainland in a private yacht. A storm got up, the boat capsized, and though the General was saved, his wife, his son and his daughter-in-law were all drowned. You can imagine the dreadful effect of such a catastrophe. General Delahaye shut himself up in his house on St. Damien and has been a recluse ever since. However, he realized that his grandchild ought to be brought up in England, in a happier and more active household, so he sent her to us."

Colvin had heard this story already, though he did not say so. Cecilia wondered whether she had made their own position sound too lowly and inferior, so she hastened to add that the General had given them a completely free hand.

"It has always been left to me to decide what is best for Henrietta; whether she should have a governess or go to school, though really, with the way she is behaving at present, I wonder if I have made the right choice."

"I feel sure you have, ma'am," he said, with unexpected force. "Nothing could be worse than a girls' boarding school, or more certain to produce bad results."

She glanced at him in surprise. "You sound very vehement, sir."

"I came across a fashionable seminary only last week. In Bath. It is kept by a very superior young woman—one of the Clares of Oxfordshire, as I was later informed in awestruck tones. She has made over a house in Belmont, spent a great deal of money on curtains and wallpaper, bought an expensive Broadwood for the children to thump, and engaged some learned female to teach them subjects they will probably not understand. Apparently she thinks that nothing further is required. The results, of course, are disastrous..."

He launched into a witty and malicious account of schoolgirls jaunting about the public places of Bath, unknown to the aristocratic Miss Clare who was too genteel to look after them properly. He exaggerated everything to make it more amusing.

Cecilia Porcheston listened and laughed and asked curiously, "What were you doing in such extraordinary surroundings, Mr. Colvin?"

He was brought up short. He could not bear to admit that his own daughter was a pupil at the school and that he had not been able to take her away. It was this humiliation that had made him so bitterly resentful. He tried to collect his thoughts, walking in the patterned shade of the chestnut trees. Their pinnacles of glossy buds stood up like candelabra.

"A connection of mine had heard good reports of the place. Once I had looked it over, I was able to inform her that it was not a suitable school for her niece."

Which was disingenuous though not absolutely untruthful.

They went into the Parsonage where Cecilia had provided a luncheon which exactly fitted the occasion: slices of cold roast beef and homebaked ham with a potato salad made to a secret recipe and flavored with anchovy sauce and mustard. And a dish of macaroons and queen cakes on the center of the table. Anything more elaborate would have seemed vulgar; she hoped to give the impression that this was their everyday fare, that she and John always drank wine and ate their cold meat off hand-painted Worcester plates.

At last the visit was over, the Weldons went away, taking Mr. Colvin with them; John set out to see one of his churchwardens, and Cecilia was left alone with nothing to do but worry about Dick Lyman.

He had left the day before. He was only going as far as Chichester, it would be cheaper than going to London and he was short of funds. His father gave him a quarterly allowance which he usually seemed to spend in the first few weeks. John said he ought to enter a profession, but what was a young man to do if he had no particular inclination? Dick said he would have liked a soldier's life, but there was no future in the army now the long war was over. He was fond of society and excelled at all field sports. Nature clearly intended him for a country gentleman. He had been a little wild in the past, but he had assured Cecilia before he left that his feelings for Henrietta were quite serious, he really was anxious to marry her and settle down.

Of course John was right, they could not have allowed the affair to continue while Henrietta was living in their house. Cecilia had felt obliged to point this out to Dick, and she thought he understood. But suppose he and Henrietta were to meet again, on neutral ground, in a place like Bath, for instance...Cecilia toyed with the idea. When

73

Henrietta eventually introduced him to her grandfather, would it not be possible to omit the fact that they had known each other previously in Sussex? Was there any risk that the old General would discover the connection between Dick and the Porchestons? Cecilia thought not. Why should he ever find out, or care if he did find out, that the late Mrs. Lyman had spent her childhood in the same Kentish village as a girl whose name had been Cecilia Phillips?

If only the young lovers could be brought together in such a way! There was one great difficulty, until today it would have seemed insuperable. How could Henrietta be maneuvered into a situation where she and Dick would be able to go on seeing each other? It was true that the General would fall in with any education suggestions that Cecilia recommended—but if Henrietta suddenly announced that she was in love, he was bound to start making inquiries, and if the school chosen for his precious grandchild turned out to be a common second-rate place where the girls were not properly guarded and chaperoned, he would blame the Porchestons for that and make trouble with Lord Midhurst. On the other hand, it would be no good sending her to the sort of strict establishment where she would be watched over by a troop of competent gorgons and where Dick would never get near her.

But ever since her talk with Mr. Colvin, a scheme had been shaping in Cecilia's mind: the prettily furnished house in Belmont, the Broadwood pianoforte, Miss Clare and her distinguished county family—it all sounded so delightfully exclusive. A school kept by a lady was just the sort of thing that would impress General Delahaye.

He himself would regard Miss Clare's birth as a kind of guarantee, and if he discovered later that Henrietta had been allowed too much freedom, he would be pained and surprised, but Cecilia did not think he would blame her for being deceived by the same illusions.

I'll drive over to Chichester tomorrow, she decided, and discuss everything with Dick. I'll tell John I want to go to the dentist. And as for sending Henrietta to school in Bath, I'll tell him a change of scene will be the quickest way to cure her broken heart.

She did not like deceiving her husband, but it was for his own good, after all. If Dick could marry Henrietta without causing them any serious trouble, the Porcheston family stood to gain in the long run. Mr. & Mrs. Richard Lyman would be valuable friends for Jack and William and little Ben, who were safe in the nursery now but would all need patrons and professions in the years ahead.

PART FOUR

Pupils and Mentors

Honor and Lucy waited in some trepidation to hear from Sally Colvin's aunt. The letter, when it came, was a pleasant surprise.

"I am indeed sorry," wrote Miss Butley, "that you should have been embarrassed and perplexed by a visit from my brother-in-law. Had I supposed that he would ever show the faintest interest in his daughter, I should have warned you what to expect. He is, of course, entitled to remove Sally if he wishes. I have tried to dissuade him, but unhappily my advice carried no weight. I consider you have acted most properly in not letting her go without consulting me first, and I can assure you that I have paid no attention to Mr. Colvin's various complaints about your school, which were clearly inspired by a petty resentment..."

"She does dislike him, doesn't she?" commented Honor with satisfaction.

Ironically, this dislike had saved the day, for if Miss Butley had really believed that her niece had been running around Bath unattended, she would have written very differently. As it was, they would lose Sally when her father sent for her, but the Butleys and Robinsons would go on recommending them among the rich families of Kensington.

Passing the open door of the schoolroom, Honor heard some interesting scraps of conversation.

"My father the Marquess is going to give me a pony phaeton for my birthday," announced Corisande. "It will be painted scarlet and gold, and I shall have two white ponies to pull it, and I shall drive around wearing a pale blue habit and a hat with a feather."

"I thought you said your father was a duke," objected Margaret.

There was a slight pause.

"Well, so he is a duke, and a marquess too."

"He can't be both."

"Of course he can."

"I don't believe you."

"That just shows how little you know about anything. Dukes have lots of other titles as well."

The argument was getting acrimonious.

"I don't know why you are always talking about your father," said Margaret. "The rest of us don't. Sally never told us anything about her father."

"I don't know anything about him to tell," said Sally. "And my aunt said he was as good as dead to us all."

"Why?" asked Margaret and Corisande in unison.

"She didn't explain why." Sally sounded puzzled.

Honor felt it was time to stop eavesdropping.

"That's enough chatter, girls!" She sailed briskly into the room. "I hope you have all learned your list of words; we are going to have a spelling lesson."

She wondered a good deal about the deplorable

Mr. Colvin. Whatever he had done or failed to do, it seemed that Sally had been kept in the dark, which removed a serious temptation, for it would have been unpardonable to question the child about her father.

They had hardly resigned themselves to losing Sally when Honor heard from a lady who wished to place her fifteen-year-old ward at a school in Bath. The letter was beautifully set out and elegantly phrased, everything about it inspired confidence, and it was delivered by hand, for the writer was staying at the Belvedere, a well-known private hotel a little further up the Lansdown Road.

Honor presented herself at the hotel. She was shown into a comfortable room where two people were just finishing breakfast. One of them rose to meet her. She was a handsome well-dressed woman not much over thirty. In spite of her youth and graceful manner, there was something a little formidable about her, and Honor was glad that she herself was still wearing black for her father; she felt this made her look older and more responsible.

"Miss Clare, how kind of you to come so soon. I am Mrs. Porcheston, and this is my ward, Henrietta Delahaye."

Henrietta stood up too, and curtsied. Honor took a good hard look at this prospective pupil. Optimistic by temperament and hoping for the best, Honor was not quite so green as she had been a few weeks ago. She realized by now that people who wanted to send girls away from home were not always perfectly frank about the reason, and she did not feel that their small community could bear the burden of another Nancy Newlander or

78

another Evelina. However, little Miss Delahaye seemed charming. Extremely pretty, she was unaffected and natural, young for her age, perhaps. A carefully brought up child who appeared sweet-tempered and amenable.

After a short conversation, Mrs. Porcheston got rid of Henrietta, sending her into the bedroom to find some patterns they were to take with them when they went shopping. Now, thought Honor, I am going to be confronted with some secret difficulty.

But there was no difficulty, merely the recital of a tragedy: the drowned parents, the heartbroken old grandfather shut up on his island.

"He wants to give Henrietta the best of everything," said Mrs. Porcheston. "We have done all we can. She has been well grounded and given the right principles, but a country village is not the place to acquire accomplishments, and with the care of a parish and five children, I have not a great deal of time to spare." Mrs. Porcheston spread her hands in a little gesture of deprecation which was not entirely natural to her, and smiled at Honor. "I thought a couple of terms in Bath would provide the polish she needs."

"Is Miss Delahaye musical?"

"Oh yes. That is, she would be, if she was better taught. That is where your judgment would be so valuable. I should leave the choice of masters entirely to you. Expense is no object."

Honor began to feel slightly light-headed.

"I ought to tell you, ma'am, that our school opened very recently, and though you may not object to our small numbers, our pupils are also rather young. The eldest is just fourteen. I don't know whether—"

"That is rather in your favor! Exactly what I should prefer. Henrietta is so delightfully young in her ways, and I don't at all fancy having her cast into a houseful of simpering misses, their heads stuffed full of sentimental nonsense. Perhaps you would give her a few little privileges, the distinction of a parlor boarder, so that she will not feel she is being relegated to the nursery."

"Yes, of course."

"You may take her to concerts, or to the play. And perhaps if any family friends should be in Bath, she might be allowed an *exeat*. Which reminds me, her cousin, Dick Lyman, may call, and there would be no objection to her seeing him. They are more like brother and sister."

As the interview drew to a close, Honor's curiosity got the better of her.

"May I ask, Mrs. Porcheston, how you came to hear of our school?"

Mrs. Porcheston answered instantly, her large eyes bright with candor. "You were recommended by Lady Midhurst. You are acquainted with her, I believe?"

Honor was not acquainted with Lady Midhurst, but she knew those who were or might be, for in the old days she and her father had lived in a world where countesses mingled freely with ordinary mortals. She could imagine what must have happened. She had sent out a good many of the printed cards to friends who still lived in that world; one of them had mentioned her to Lady Midhurst, who had passed on her name to Mrs. Porcheston. This was the way that Honor had always hoped news of the school would spread. General Delahaye's grandchild was an acquisition and there would be others to follow, they had only to be patient.

She walked down the hill to Belmont treading on air.

The following afternoon Henrietta arrived, accompanied by her guardian. Although Mrs. Porcheston had decided on the school without seeing it, Honor and Lucy naturally wanted to make a good impression, so it was a little unfortunate that Evelina had one of her attacks of Going Off on the staircase and fell down the last few steps just as the front door was opened. Evelina lay with her head against the newel post and her eyes rolling, looking absolutely half-witted. Luckily Mrs. Porcheston did not seem to grasp her condition and thought this was an ordinary childish tumble. Vaguely benign, she said that she hoped the little girl had not bumped herself too badly. Honor suspected she must be rather shortsighted.

The young heiress settled in very easily. This was a relief, for many girls might have resented being sent to boarding school at the advanced age of fifteen. Henrietta did not seem to mind in the least. Although she had a room to herself—there was still space and to spare—she invited the others to come in, let them handle all her belongings, and showed an artless pleasure when they liked everything so much. Even Corisande was charmed and the Marlows were round eyed with wonder. They had never seen anything so pretty as her rosewood writing case, with the inlaid figure of Mercury on the lid, her two china birds which she promptly put on the mantel shelf, her shell-encrusted workbox, her cameo brooch and necklace of seed pearls. While as for her clothes, though

81

simple and youthful, they were quite exquisite.

"Fancy having all these white dresses," murmured Martha, reverently fingering the pile of almost transparent muslin, each crisp layer traced and shadowed by a different pattern of stripes or sprigs or dots.

"Yes, there are far too many. Would you like one?" asked Henrietta.

"Oh, I could not!" exclaimed Martha, flushing and withdrawing her hand. "I have nothing to give you in exchange."

She knew the etiquette relating to schoolgirl presents, and anyway, one could hardly accept a dress!

Honor took the last pair of shoes out of the trunk and said, "You cannot give your dresses away, Henrietta."

"Then can I lend her one, Miss Clare? We are nearly the same height. Surely there can be no harm in that?"

Honor saw the longing in Martha's eyes. Her limp cambric was so skimpy it would soon have to be handed on to Margaret, and she had nothing more presentable. It would be cruel to refuse.

"Henrietta has a generous nature," she said later, justifying herself to Lucy. "She made the offer without the smallest hint of superiority or condescension. That is a frame of mind one ought to encourage."

"So long as Martha does not become unsettled and discontented. Not that I think she will, poor child. She seems almost too uncomplaining."

"I am so sorry for those three girls. How their parents could go off and leave them without any proper provision—I suppose Mr. Marlow was in some sort of trouble, but even so it seems quite heartless. I'm glad Martha can enjoy wearing a pretty dress, even a borrowed one."

Everyone liked Henrietta, except Nancy, who liked nobody. Having come off worst in her clash with Honor, she had lost her nerve and her impetus for causing trouble. She went about scowling dismally, ate and slept a great deal and learned nothing. Honor and Lucy felt concerned about her but could not break down her hostility. At least she was no longer subverting the younger girls. As a daring rebel she had a dangerous attraction for Margaret and Sally, but once she lapsed into sulking she ceased to have any influence over them.

So the school was now running more smoothly. They were well into May, all the pale walls of Bath were drenched in sunlight, all the trees in the city shining with fresh young leaves, and the hanging woods below Beechen Cliff were shady and enticing.

Every day Honor or Lucy took the girls for a long walk. They were returning along Alfred Street one afternoon when an elegantly dressed gentleman on the opposite pavement took off his hat and made Honor a slight bow. For the first moment she did not recognize him. He crossed the road and Sally gave a shriek of delight.

"Papa!"

And like the frog prince in the fairy tale, the elegant gentleman was transformed into Mr. Marcus Colvin. Honor could hardly believe her eyes.

That dreadful violet garment had vanished, and in its place he wore a superbly cut swallowtail coat of dark blue superfine, which fitted so well that he no longer looked stocky or bulky, but extremely muscular and well proportioned. Even his skin was not as swarthy as she remembered, and he had been to a good barber.

"Papa, where have you been?" demanded Sally, catching his hand.

"To see you, but you were not at home. I'll come again in the morning, if that is convenient." He looked inquiringly at Honor.

"Certainly, Mr. Colvin," she said, collecting her wits. He would want to remove Sally. A pity, but it couldn't be helped.

The little girl danced around him, saying, "Why can't you come back with us now? Where are you going?"

"It is not very polite to keep on asking people where they have been and where they are going, as I'm sure Miss Clare must have told you," he said, giving Honor quite a friendly smile.

His light, greenish gray eyes were not nearly so catlike as she remembered, and not really too close together.

She said, "I'm afraid I haven't succeeded in curbing her curiosity."

"I dare say it is an uphill struggle."

The words died away. He was no longer looking at her, but at something just behind her left shoulder. She turned to see what it was that had caught his attention. He was staring at Henrietta Delahaye.

Henrietta was an unusually pretty girl. She was the only one of their eight pupils who drew much notice from strangers, for Martha was gawky and rather plain, while the others were still very young. Honor and Lucy had decided that they would have to keep a special watch over Henrietta. Luckily she was not a coquette, did not seem to realize the interest she aroused, and met

84

bold glances with a dreamy, far away innocence. At the moment she was talking to poor, slow-witted Evelina who had been startled by a barking dog. She was always very kind to Evelina.

Marcus Colvin was gazing at her as though he had seen a vision.

"Well, we must not stand about any longer," said Honor in a brisk, governessy voice. "Good afternoon, Mr. Colvin."

As they moved on, she had a picture of herself from the outside; an uninteresting female drably dressed in black, forced into middle age at twenty-four and trailing about Bath with a pack of schoolgirls. That was how Colvin must see her. If he saw her at all. He was probably too dazzled by Henrietta. She wondered what he was doing now, but would not look round. Until she found that one of her charges was missing. Then she did turn. Henrietta was some yards behind them, talking to Mr. Colvin.

"Henrietta, come here at once!" Honor called out sharply.

Henrietta hurried to join them.

"What was Sally's father saying to you?"

"Nothing to signify. He wanted to know my name."

"Did he say anything else?"

"He didn't have time, Miss Clare."

"And just as well," Honor commented grimly, describing the scene to Lucy.

"I should be sorry to think he was that sort of man. I imagine he is coming tomorrow to tell us that he wants to take Sally away."

"Yes, and we had better see him together or I expect I shall be rude to him again."

But when Mr. Colvin called on them, it was to

85

say, with a slightly apologetic air, that he would be grateful if they could keep Sally a little longer. He had not yet been able to make adequate arrangements for her.

Of course, they agreed, neither of them wanted to part with Sally. It crossed Honor's mind that he could save money by leaving his daughter where she was. Her fees had been paid, and his tailor probably hadn't.

He made some neutral remark about the school, adding: "I see you now have General Delahaye's granddaughter here."

Honor was astonished by his impudence. What concern was it of his? And how could he be certain, incidentally, that Henrietta was the General's grandchild? Or was it simply a bow at a venture? Having learned her surname, was he trying to find out whether or not she was the heiress of the wealthy old recluse with his great estates in the Scilly Isles and elsewhere?

Lucy made an evasive answer and Honor ignored the question altogether, saying, "If you are going to leave Sally with us, sir, we must have your address. I'll make a note of it."

"No need to do that, Miss Clare; you won't forget it. I am staying in Bath at present, putting up at the York Hotel."

"I never heard of such a piece of effrontery!" burst out Honor as soon as he had gone. "Leaving Sally with us, after all he said about the school, and staying on in Bath himself so that he can try to scrape up an acquaintance with Henrietta, I suppose. No doubt that is his profession: marrying heiresses. He must be three times her age, it is quite disgusting."

"You are exaggerating, Honor. He can't be

much over thirty-five. I agree it is odd that he should be so interested in Henrietta, but otherwise he seems perfectly respectable. You are letting your prejudices run away with you."

Honor would not admit this, though privately she knew it was true. She was in a quandary over Mr. Colvin. She had started out by disliking him because he had been rude to her and critical of the school (two excellent reasons). She had also taken him for the sort of vulgar upstart with whom she did not wish to associate. Now that she had seen him dressed so differently, she realized that she had been wrong. This was humiliating. A lady ought to be able to recognize a gentleman anywhere, whatever he was wearing. Marcus Colvin had made a fool of her and she held this against him. He might be a gentleman by birth but he had not behaved like a gentleman, turning up in that awful coat and confusing her. It flattered her self-esteem to believe that he was up to no good.

He came frequently to the school, in order to take Sally out. He never mentioned Henrietta, but he didn't need to. He had Sally to act as his innocent spy within the gates. It was an uneasy situation.

After a week of this, Honor said: "I think perhaps, Mr. Colvin, you ought not to take Sally out so often. It is distracting for her and the other girls are inclined to be envious."

"I am sorry about that. Perhaps she could bring a friend with her next time. I have been meaning to ask."

You must take me for a complete simpleton, thought Honor. She smiled sweetly, saying, "How very kind of you. Perhaps she could invite Margaret Marlow or Corisande Bilting, they are the nearest to her in age—"

"What name did you say?"

"Margaret Marlow? She is one of three sisters whose parents have gone to India—".

"No, no—the other one: Bilting. Is that little Miss Buttercup with her nose in the air? Of course, one can see the likeness. My dear Miss Clare, however did you come to take her as a pupil at your select establishment?"

"Her mother sent her to us in the ordinary way," said Honor repressively. "They live in London, in a very good part of the town."

"Yes, I know. Hertford Street, exceedingly fashionable. Antoinette Bilting is one of the most expensive courtesans in London."

This was a thunderbolt. Surely he could not be serious? But she could see he was. He had hesitated over the word courtesan, as though he had intended to use another. Not that it made any difference, she knew exactly what he meant.

"I don't believe you," she said automatically, though without much hope, because she had begun to believe him almost at once, thinking of Mrs. Bilting's effusive style and florid handwriting, of Corisande's clothes, a little too costly somehow and lacking the infallible simplicity of Henrietta's. And (good heavens) all those stories of imaginary dukes and marquesses, only they weren't imaginary, they were all too real and probably Corisande didn't know which of them was her father.

"You will have to get rid of her if you want the school to survive," said Marcus Colvin.

He was standing with one shoulder against the

white marble mantelpiece, gazing thoughtfully at his gleaming Hessians.

Honor collected her wits. "I thought it was your opinion that the school is bound to fail. And why should I send the poor child away? She is not to blame for her mother's situation. She is doing no harm here."

"You try telling the other parents that. Her presence may not cause any difficulties now, but think ahead a little. What careful mama is going to welcome Corisande Bilting as a bosom friend for her precious daughter of fourteen or fifteen?"

"I don't see why they should object," argued Honor, who saw quite well. "And as you are removing Sally very shortly, you need not be afraid that she will be corrupted."

(2)

"I don't understand," said Lucy. "How could such an improper person ever come to hear of our school?"

"I sent out cards to a great many of my old friends, and I can only suppose that one of them has a husband who visits this fashionable trollop."

"Oh, surely not!"

"I don't know what you mean by *surely not*," said Honor rather snappishly. "Mr. Colvin seems to know all about her."

"Yes, but you are forever insisting that he is an improper person himself."

Honor changed the subject. "So do you think we ought to get rid of Corisande?"

"Good gracious, no! She is not to blame for her mother's errors. I dare say the poor woman longs for her daughter to lead a different sort of life. That is probably why she sent her to us."

"More likely she hoped Corisande would make some genteel friends."

"I dare say you are right," Lucy sighed. "At any rate, it would be most unchristian to turn her away. Only think, Honor, we have this opportunity of molding her character and entirely changing the pattern of her future. How can we refuse such a sacred trust?"

Honor wondered how much influence Lucy's noble sentiments would have on Corisande, who seemed such a worldly little person. Still, she deserved the chance of a good upbringing. How else could a girl in her situation be expected to escape the trap of history repeating itself? (They must try to dissuade her from talking so much about the dukes.)

Honor had a great deal on her mind, what with Henrietta and the Colvins, Corisande, the expenses of housekeeping, and even Evelina. Here there was something to be pleased with. Evelina was very much better. Honor had taught her to do simple knotting and she spent most of her time making yards of fringe. This seemed to concentrate her faculties, she looked less stupid and had fewer fits. The problem of the Marlows, Honor pushed into the background. It would not become acute until they needed more clothes or a summer holiday. Nancy's mute inertia had lulled her into a state of false security. Until the day they went to buy her some new shoes.

Honor had written to Mrs. Newlander, asking permission to do this as her others were becoming too small. She added, as tactfully as she could manage, that although Nancy had now settled down, she did not seem very happy and was slow at her lessons. Mrs. Newlander replied instantly, authorizing Honor to buy anything that was needed and betraying her astonishment that Nancy was not once again being sent home in disgrace.

"If she is fairly quiet and not too great a trouble, that is as much as we expected. I fear that a cheerful disposition and an improved mind are too much to hope for. I must own that Nancy has been a sad trial to us from the hour of her birth."

Sad trial or not, Nancy was a growing girl and the discomfort of tight shoes might make her even more disagreeable.

They walked down the Lansdown Road in silence.

"What kind of shoes would you like, Nancy?" Honor tried to make something of the occasion.

"I don't care," said Nancy indifferently.

In George Street they had to wait for a break in the broad stream of traffic, standing opposite the York Hotel. As it happened, Mr. Colvin had just finished breakfast and was looking out of the window. He observed Honor and Nancy with the thoughtful air of a naturalist studying two rather rare insects. Luckily Honor did not know this; it would have annoyed her. Mr. Colvin laid down his newspaper and decided to go out.

In Milsom Street there were a great many shoppers and saunterers, and Honor had gone only a few yards when she found herself facing someone she knew.

"My dear Lizzie!" she exclaimed. "What a surprise! How long have you been in Bath? Why didn't you let me know?"

"Dearest Honor—not very long. And my time has been so entirely occupied."

Lizzie Chapman was a few years older than Honor, her husband had been killed at Waterloo. She had often stayed at Walbury in the old days, in fact she had angled for invitations to the Clares' convivial house parties, for she hated being a widow and was eagerly waiting to be consoled. Honor had written to tell her about the school but she had not replied. Now she sounded defensive.

"You know what a shocking correspondent I am. The trouble is, one needs a whole morning to write a letter that is worth reading, and a whole morning is something I never seem to have at my disposal. How brave of you to start your own school. You always were an original, Honor—we used to say it was your Irish blood. Is that one of your pupils?"

"Yes," said Honor briefly. She wished she could have had Henrietta or Sally with her. Any of the others (except Evelina) would have been preferable to slouching Nancy. To do her justice, Nancy had effaced herself by moving aside and pretending to gaze into a shop window. Lizzie eyed her curiously.

"I cannot imagine you surrounded by a gaggle of schoolgirls. Are you horridly strict?"

"You had better come and find out. We are not two minutes' walk from the Upper Rooms."

"That would be charming," said Lizzie insincerely. "Though I cannot promise precisely when— I am so very much engaged with Lady Sophia. And the Ackroyds are here—you remember the Ackroyds? Now the weather is getting so stuffy in Bath, we think of all moving on to Lyme."

She brought the conversation to an end in a

torrent of nervous effusiveness, and Honor was glad to see her go. She had not realized what an embarrassment she had become to her friends: poor Honor Clare who had fallen on hard times and was obliged to teach in a school. They would have liked it better if she had stayed on at Walbury with Sidney and Euphemia, then they could have thought of her complacently, living in her old home under the protection of her relations. Setting up a school, and in Bath of all places, was the sort of selfish scheme that involved one's friends in the awkwardness of deciding whether they still were one's friends or not. So very uncomfortable, for them, she thought bitterly.

Shrugging off the whole episode, she looked round for Nancy, and was surprised to find that she had gone into the shop.

It was a superior haberdasher's, kept by one Josiah Pledge who also described himself as a glover and hosier. Peeping through the slanted panes of the bow window, Honor could see clearly into the highly polished interior. Most of the goods were displayed on shelves behind the high mahogany counter. A woman in a gray dress was attending to a seated customer, Nancy was standing a little apart with her back to the half-open door.

As she went in Honor heard the woman in charge singing the praise of a pair of expensive white stockings.

"Part of our latest consignment from Paris, ma'am."

"But they are not at all what I want," bleated the customer.

Nancy was apparently inspecting the skeins of colored silk in a glass-fronted cabinet against the wall. Close to her, on the end of the counter, there was a tray containing pincushions, needle-cases, thimbles and other small items. While she went on gazing at the silks without turning her head, Honor was horrified to see her left hand slide out towards the tray, from which she neatly abstracted a small pair of embroidery scissors.

"Nancy!" she exclaimed.

"Oh, Miss Clare!" Nancy started violently.

At the same moment the woman behind the counter said, "You thieving little wretch! You took something from the counter—give it over this instant."

"I didn't! I didn't!" protested Nancy, frightened now, and backing towards Honor.

The woman called to someone at the back of the shop.

"Mr. Pledge, come here, will you. I've caught a thief."

A red-faced man came hurrying in. "What's all this about? What has been taken?"

Honor began to say weakly, "I think there has been some mistake."

She could actually feel Nancy beside her trembling with fear. Nancy, who had seemed so large and threatening, like an untamed animal, was now reduced to a terrified child—she was after all only thirteen. Honor very much disliked the expression of the shopkeeper's hard eyes and tight mouth. He was still demanding to know what had been taken.

The woman said, "Something out of the tray. I saw it flash as she moved her hand."

They both peered down at the tray. No one was looking at Honor or Nancy. The reluctant stocking buyer had left the shop.

Hardly moving her lips, Honor whispered to Nancy, "Give it to me."

Nancy shot her a sidelong glance of uncomprehending terror. Then she pushed something cold and narrow towards Honor, who let it drop into her shopping basket.

A second later Mr. Pledge announced: "A pair of scissors! There is a pair of scissors wanting." He turned on Nancy. "Give them back at once, you wicked hussy. It's no manner of use you pretending you took them by accident. I mean to have the law on you and there will be plenty for you to snivel about when you are transported to Botany Bay."

Nancy gulped. She had been petrified into stupidity and had no clear idea what to do next.

Honor said, "You have not got the scissors, have you, Nancy? Show us your hands and let us see that you have nothing to hide."

Silently uncurling her fingers with their short, bitten nails, Nancy held out her empty hands.

The shopkeeper was disappointed, but his assistant plucked at his sleeve, muttering ominously, and then they both looked at Honor. For the first time she grasped the danger of her own position. Impulsively she had rescued Nancy, only to become suspected as her accomplice. The scissors were in her basket, whose wicker handles seemed to burn her arm as she stood there cold with sweat, wondering desperately, how am I to get out of this? What am I to do?

She and Nancy were only a few inches apart, they had given away the fact that they knew each other (a stupid mistake) and the shopkeeper must have guessed what had become of the stolen scissors.

"Let me see the contents of your basket."

It was a demand, not a request.

"I shall do no such thing. What you are suggesting is quite outrageous."

Her indignation sounded feeble and unconvincing.

"Then I must detain you while we summon a law officer."

Wouldn't that be even worse? Once the law was invoked, the man would have to prosecute. Suppose Honor admitted the truth now and offered him money? Only he seemed so anxious to bring a charge and she was no longer able to think rationally. As she stood there in a state of dumb panic, she heard a movement near the doorway of the shop.

A man's voice asked, "Are you interested in selling your wares or are you not? How much longer must I wait to be served?"

Honor's spine prickled.

The shopkeeper was all ingratiating smiles.

"I beg your pardon, sir. We have just apprehended two criminals—caught them in the act. The young woman here and her child confederate have filched a valuable item from this tray."

"Indeed?" Marcus Colvin thrust his way between Honor and Nancy to inspect the tray with an air of cool disdain. "I should not have thought there was much worth stealing," he remarked with the calculated rudeness he had mastered so well.

Only Honor knew that when he brushed past her he had slipped a hand inside her basket and that the scissors were no longer there.

The shopkeeper began to gobble and protest. His goods were all of the first quality, he could not afford to be robbed. Colvin leaned negligently on the counter, seemingly bored by this harangue. He glanced around him.

"What's that over there on the floor?"

"Where?" Mr. Pledge and his assistant both craned to see.

"Behind the chair."

Colvin approached the chair where the elderly lady had been sitting. He stooped and appeared to pick something up. He had taken care to place himself in such a way that he was blocking the view of the two shop people. When he turned he was holding out the delicate little pair of embroidery scissors, made of Sheffield steel, with the handle gilded and engraved.

Pledge gave a cry of something like anguish.

"Is this what all the fuss has been about?" asked Colvin in pretended astonishment. "A storm in a teacup indeed. I think you had better apologize to the young lady."

He had not glanced once in Honor's direction before this, and did so now with the bland civility of a complete stranger.

The shopkeeper was positively servile; it was a dreadful thing to have accused a perfectly respectable young lady of theft and she might ruin him if she chose. Between his fulsome apologies he cast vindictive glances at his assistant, whom he blamed for the mistake. He now thought that the previous customer must have picked up the scissors and then knocked them off the counter without noticing. The woman was dissatisfied and puzzled; she was sure she had seen Nancy take something from the tray—but Nancy had been nowhere near the chair and nothing else was missing. Almost stunned with relief, Honor felt dimly sorry for them both.

As she and Nancy left the shop, Mr. Colvin was critically examining a pair of gloves.

Milsom Street was almost too much for her: the brightness and the rush of warm air, the shifting color of the women's dresses, she felt as though they had really been let out of a cage. Nancy stumbled and Honor caught her arm.

"Do you feel faint?"

"I feel sick," said Nancy.

The shoes forgotten, they made for home.

Walking very slowly, they had only just turned into George Street when Mr. Colvin overtook them.

He grasped Honor firmly by the elbow. "You'd better come into the hotel. You don't look fit to go another step."

"I am perfectly well, but I think Nancy ought to sit down. It is very kind of you—and as for what you did just now, I cannot thank you enough . . ."

Mr. Colvin bundled them through the august doorway of the York Hotel; they must have looked an ill-assorted trio to the servants and the guests who were coming and going in the hall. Commanding a waiter to bring coffee and brandy, he took them into a small, rather airless room containing a great many chairs upholstered in a violent shade of red. Nancy collapsed into one of the chairs, and Honor instructed her to put her head down and she would feel better.

"You aren't going to be sick, are you?" she asked anxiously.

"Not now."

Honor turned to Mr. Colvin and tried once again to thank him.

"You saved us from a horrid situation and I am exceedingly grateful. And it was so clever of you; how did you know—"

"I was watching through the shop window. It is quite unnecessary for you to thank me. I took no serious risk of being found out. What you did was quixotic to the point of lunacy. Has this miserable brat thanked you yet? Too busy feeling sorry for herself, I take it. Hey, you! What's your name, Nancy—have you thanked Miss Clare for saving you from the results of your criminal folly?"

"She didn't do it for me," muttered Nancy. "She only wanted to prevent a scandal that would disgrace her school."

"Now you listen to me," said Colvin, and Nancy cowered back into her chair, he sounded so fierce. "And try to use what wits God gave you. No doubt Miss Clare sets a high value on her school, but she is not likely to sacrifice her life to preserve it. Even if the place closed down tomorrow, she would not be anywhere near to ruin: a young woman of character with energy and determination, friends and property, her whole future before her. She could easily have left you to sink while she survived. Instead she tried to protect you and was herself in great danger of being arrested and perhaps hanged."

"Hanged?" faltered Nancy.

"No, no!" interrupted Honor. "It is cruel to frighten her so. Mr. Colvin is exaggerating, Nancy. At the worst I might have been transported to Australia."

"A charming alternative," he remarked. "And what would you have done when you got there?

99

Opened a seminary for the daughters of convicts, I dare say."

Honor would have liked to hit him, but she was confused by her deep sense of obligation, and by the surprising way he had described her. And Nancy was asking a question.

"Did you truly do it for me?"

Honor was not at all sure why she had taken the incriminating scissors and hidden them. She had acted from pure instinct, but it must have been an instinct to protect this difficult but terrified and vulnerable girl, for she had not thought once about the reputation of the school.

She said, "I didn't want you to go to prison."

"Why not? You hate me, everybody does. You said you'd have me put in a madhouse."

"Well, I may have said so, but I didn't do it," retorted Honor, caught between guilt and exasperation. (I ought to be in a madhouse myself, she decided.) "Of course I don't hate you. We should all like you very much if only you would try a little harder to like us."

Nancy burst into tears. She rolled about in the fat upholstery of the chair, and the more Honor tried to comfort her, the more noisily she cried. Most of what she said was incoherent, what did come through was strangely disturbing. No one had ever wanted to like her before, Papa and Mama would have been glad to have her transported and out of the way. Honor glanced at Mr. Colvin, who rang the bell imperiously.

A waiter appeared at last with their refreshments. Mr. Colvin poured out three cups of strong coffee and picked up the bottle.

"I don't want any brandy," said Honor.

"Well, I do," he said frankly.

When they were all somewhat restored and Honor was ready to take Nancy home, he insisted that they were not fit to walk up the hill and ordered two chairs. So they returned to Belmont in a stately procession, each in her glass-fronted box with a couple of sturdy chairmen to carry the poles, like two Bath ladies going to a ball.

Arriving in this unexpected way, they caused a good deal of excitement at the school. Honor let Nancy go upstairs, while she gave Lucy a true account of what had happened and told everyone else an unconvincing story about Nancy being overcome by the heat.

Presently she went to take off her bonnet. She sat at her dressing table and stared at herself in the oval looking glass she had brought from Walbury, the glass that had for years reflected her wide bedroom there with the Chinese wallpaper, and her own carefree image, in a succession of gauze dresses or pretty hats. Now it reflected her small town bedroom and the face of a woman who might have been tried, found guilty, and sent half across the world on one of those terrible convict ships, for helping to steal a pair of scissors. Could that have happened to her? She scarcely believed it.

There was a tap on the door, and Nancy came in carrying a small collection of objects which she laid down on the dressing table.

"What am I to do with these, Miss Clare?"

"What are they?" asked Honor. And guessed immediately what they were.

A pinchbeck bracelet, a green enamel vinaigrette, a spray of artificial cherries.

"Nancy, do you mean to say you've stolen these things too? Since you've been in Bath?"

"Yes. Only now I think perhaps I ought not to keep them."

"But how did you get hold of them?" This was really appalling.

"It was quite easy. I can always pick up something when you or Miss Fielder take us into the shops to spend our pocket money. Especially if it is Miss Fielder, she is much less noticing than you are."

Good God, thought Honor, she might have been caught any time. We've been sitting on a volcano all these weeks. If Mr. Colvin knew how right he was about our incompetence!

"I simply don't understand. You have your own pocket money." For the Newlanders had not been mean. "You can buy what you like, within reason."

"I never really wanted any of this stuff. It was the excitement. An adventure."

And in fact one couldn't imagine Nancy buying any of these things. Or a pair of embroidery scissors; she was no great needlewoman. The little hoard had the random look of oddments found in a jackdaw's nest. Had Nancy really taken them out of sheer bravado? There must be more to it than that. Honor began to speak to her very seriously. The stealing would have to stop.

"You may have felt very clever so long as no one caught you, but you didn't like it when they did."

"It was horrid." Nancy shivered. "And anyway it all seems silly now. I can't think why I did it."

There was a lot about Nancy that was hard to understand. Remembering some of the things that had slipped out when she was off her guard, Honor probed delicately. It was plain that the wretched girl had always felt unloved and unwanted at home. This was strange, for she was an eldest child, and they were usually welcome. There was a sister born a year later who was a pet and favorite, and several younger brothers. The family sounded happy enough, only Nancy was a misfit. It was a vicious circle probably; a cross, whining baby who irritated her parents, and gradually becoming aware of this, turned into a contrary, resentful child. She is more to be pitied than condemned, thought Honor. We must do what we can for her. And in the meantime, how am I to dispose of her ill-gotten gains?

"We can hardly return them to the shops," she said. "That would lead to a great many awkward questions."

"I thought you might sell them and give the money to the poor."

"Oh, did you? And how am I to set about selling them? Stand in the street in a red petticoat like an old peddler woman, perhaps?"

This made Nancy laugh. Her whole expression changed. She would be quite a pleasant looking girl if she laughed more often.

(3)

Honor's feelings about Marcus Colvin were once again wildly confused. She was not only extremely grateful for the way he had come to her rescue, she had been amazed by the speed of his response, his deviousness and his skill. He really had been remarkably quick-witted, as though he was used to dealing with such dangerous situations. How cleverly he had tricked the shopkeeper by pretending to find the scissors on the floor.

103

"Do you think he might be a cardsharper?" she asked Lucy.

"Who might be a cardsharper?"

When Honor explained, Lucy looked at her rather oddly, and said, "You think a great deal about Mr. Colvin, don't you?"

"Certainly not! I never think of him at all. Well, that is to say, he did get me out of an awkward scrape, and one cannot help wondering why he does such peculiar things."

"And he is the only man you ever meet. It doesn't suit you to spend your life surrounded by females. I am so accustomed to it myself, I did not consider how trying you would find it. I do wish our circle of acquaintance was a little wider. Perhaps you will meet some interesting people at Mrs. Foster's this evening."

Honor was rather insulted by the suggestion that she was the kind of woman who could not live without men. The small, enclosed feminine world of the school was certainly very different from anything she had known before, but she had become happily absorbed in it; all she missed and sometimes longed for was the solitude and freedom of her old life at Walbury, before the arrival of Sydney and Euphemia. If she ever seemed restless, it was for that, not for any acquaintances or society she might meet at the Fosters' or elsewhere.

Mrs. Foster was the married sister of Mr. French the lawyer. He and his family had introduced Honor and Lucy into Bath society. As they could not both leave the school at the same time, they took turns to accept such invitations as came their way.

The company in Cavendish Place that evening

was made up of local residents of the first and second strata: members of the landed gentry who found that life in Bath agreed with them, officers on half pay, professional men with their wives and daughters. There seemed to Honor to be an unduly large proportion of clergymen and widows. She herself had now gone from black into half mourning and wore a dress of soft lavender color and a very pretty lace cap. One of the clergymen immediately began to make himself agreeable. It was a pity that she found him affected and insipid. The drawing room was crowded, and so many people standing close together in each other's shadows seemed to blot out the light of the candles. Eventually she managed to get rid of the parson by sitting down on the only vacant chair.

She found herself next to a formidable lady in olive green crepe, who said, categorically, "You are Miss Clare and you have opened a school in Belmont."

Honor admitted that this was true.

"I am Miss Barnstable."

"How do you do, ma'am. I am very glad to meet you."

Miss Barnstable kept one of the most successful seminaries in Bath. Nearly forty little girls were being transformed into young ladies at her superior establishment in Queen Square. She asked several searching questions which Honor answered cautiously, for although her interest sounded perfectly well-meaning, there were some things one would rather not give away.

"Eight pupils," commented Miss Barnstable. "That is an ambitious start."

Honor wondered if this was ironic, decided that

it was not, and asked, "How many did you start with, ma'am?"

"Only two."

"Two! But surely that cannot have been sufficient for . . ." She broke off, afraid that a reference to profit might be considered impertinent, if not vulgar.

"My school grew out of circumstance rather than design. We had an empty room after my brother married, and I was asked to take charge of two young girls whose parents were in the West Indies. My old governess was still with us; gradually other children came to share their lessons. One thing led to another, until we were obliged to leave Gay Street and move to a larger house."

So that is how one ought to start a school, thought Honor: by taking a paying pupil or two into a household that already exists in its own right. Lucy and I were not able to do that.

"I suppose you now have many more applicants than you have places for," she said a little enviously.

"That is so." Miss Barnstable was complacent. "I take very good care whom I accept, and if you are wise you will do the same. Always insist on references and always make sure you are paid a full year's fees in advance when the parents are expecting to go abroad. You will be surprised at the shifts people will get up to, if they think you can be taken in."

Honor thanked her for her advice, without adding that she had been unpleasantly surprised several times already. She wondered briefly what Miss Barnstable would have done about Nancy. Five other schools had apparently found her intractable and unteachable, and her present mood of responsive gratitude might wear off. Determined to keep her, Honor realized that this could be yet another mistake.

It was not late when she returned to Belmont and there was still a light burning in the parlor, where she found Lucy and Henrietta entertaining an exceptionally good-looking young man.

"Miss Clare, this is Dick!" announced Henrietta, flushed and inexplicit.

The young man stood up. He was slim, with aquiline features, and tall enough to gaze down at Honor with a charming smile which made her feel glad that for once she was not looking like a schoolmistress.

"I hope you don't mind my calling, ma'am."

"This is Henrietta's cousin, Mr. Lyman," explained Lucy. "He arrived in Bath this evening."

Young Mr. Lyman went on making himself agreeable. A few minutes conversation convinced Honor that most of his charm was on the surface, there was probably no great depth of sensibility or intelligence. Still, one could not have everything, and it was a pleasure to see anyone so well worth looking at. Remembering Mrs. Porcheston's instructions, she invited him to go with them to a concert the following evening. This obviously pleased both the cousins. According to Mrs. Porcheston, they regarded each other as brother and sister. Honor could not be sure about the young man; but she was pretty certain that Henrietta's emotions were more than sisterly. However, it hardly mattered. Mrs. Porcheston had gone out of her way to make it clear that they might be allowed to meet. Honor knew that there were no male Delahayes left to succeed the General and it was quite likely that he hoped eventually to make a match between his granddaughter and this very presentable young man who was in some way related to them.

Next day was Sally's birthday. Her father brought her a most unusual present that delighted her: the costume of a Turkish lady, small enough for her to wear, and including a long, diaphanous veil, a gold-embroidered tunic, and a pair of wide pantaloons made from yards and yards of the finest and most lustrous orange silk—a garment that an oriental lady would wear instead of a skirt.

Sally hugged her father impulsively.

"Did you bring it back with you on the ship, Papa?"

Honor was examining the fine leather slippers. Back from where, she wondered. This was the first mention she had heard of a ship.

"Yes," said Mr. Colvin, "and you are lucky to get it, for practically everything I had was ruined by seawater when we lost our mast in the storm. By the time I landed at Plymouth it was a choice between disguising myself as a fugitive from a pasha's harem or wearing the coat I got in Sicily which Miss Clare admires so much."

"You are teasing, Papa! You know you could not get into any of these clothes. And how do you know Miss Clare admires your Sicilian coat? Did she tell you?"

"No, but she used to look at it in a very particular way that I am sure denoted admiration."

Honor, scarlet with embarrassment, said, "If you want to show your costume to the other girls, Sally, you can go and put it on now."

Sally ran off calling Corisande and Marianne to come and help her dress up, and Honor was left alone with Mr. Colvin.

"How was I to know that you'd been abroad and lost your baggage?"

"Please don't apologize, Miss Clare."

"I wasn't going to," she retorted, suppressing her chagrin as best she could. He knew as well as she did that she had drawn several wrong conclusions about him, merely from the way he had been dressed.

She wondered how she could have been so stupid. Even his coloring did not seem unduly dark, and she realized, having now a clue, that his skin must have been burned brown by the sun, that was why he had looked so foreign.

"How long were you abroad?" she asked.

"Three years."

"In Turkey?"

"In the Ottoman Empire. That includes Greece, you know." He changed the subject. "I have a scheme to put to you. Can I persuade you and Miss Fielder to let me take you all—the whole school—for a picnic in the country on Saturday to celebrate Sally's birthday?"

"How very kind of you. Are you sure you want to burden yourself with such a party?"

"Of course I do. And Sally would like it above all things."

There could be no reason to refuse. It was a generous offer, even if he was hoping to get something out of it. Like the chance of making friends with Henrietta. Honor had a sudden idea.

"I wonder if we might bring Miss Delahaye's cousin with us?"

He looked surprised and rather interested.

"Has Miss Delahaye a cousin in Bath? Yes, by all means bring her too."

Honor thanked him but did not pursue the matter. She had not intended to mislead him; if he took it for granted that Henrietta's cousin was a girl, he would soon find out his mistake.

Dick Lyman said he would be delighted to come to the picnic. He had his curricle with him, might he drive his cousin? Honor thought she could allow this, provided they kept with the rest of the party.

The great day dawned gray and misty, to the dismay of the younger girls, who had been awake literally since dawn, peering out at the overcast sky. Lucy pointed out that a dull morning often meant a fine day, and sure enough, by the time prayers and breakfast were over, the sun had broken through. At eleven the hired carriages were at the door, an open barouche which Mr. Colvin was driving himself and a two-horse landau driven by a postilion. It took some time to get everyone settled, and while the postilion was taking down the head of the landau, Dick Lyman came dashing up in a smart curricle and Henrietta ran to greet him.

"Who's that fellow?" demanded Colvin.

"That," said Honor, "is Miss Delahaye's cousin."

At last they were ready to leave. Honor had elected to travel in the landau at the back of the cavalcade, with Nancy, Evelina and Margaret. Occasionally, as they inched their way through the crowded streets, she caught a glimpse of Dick and Henrietta perched high in the curricle and talking with animation. More rarely, at the head of their procession, she saw Mr. Colvin on the box of the barouche, his hat tilted to a rakish angle and Sally bouncing excitedly beside him.

Once across the Avon at Pulteney Bridge they went spinning along at a much faster pace, took the Warminster Road and soon left the streets and houses of Bath behind them. A country drive was a great pleasure to Honor, she had never before spent so long mewed up in a town. Presently they came to a wooded valley where everything was green and shining in the morning light: grass, trees and hedges, and the serene stillness of the opposite hillside. Marcus Colvin had surveyed the ground a few days earlier and chosen a suitable field for his picnic.

"No cows and hardly a thistle in sight," he informed them. "I hope you approve."

They did approve. The girls jumped out of the carriages, breathing in the country air and stretching their young bodies in so much free space. Soon Nancy was swinging on a gate, Margaret and Sally were tossing a ball about, Martha was walking down the field, head bent, searching for wild flowers in the grass. Evelina and little Marianne frisked like puppies. Corisande held back at first, a town-bred child, pretty as a doll, not wanting to dirty her hands or crease her dress. Then Nancy called her and she ran towards the gate.

Only fifteen-year-old Henrietta was left hesitating between the two groups: the children playing and the elders occupying themselves with the carriages, horses and picnic hampers. In the end she stayed with them.

Mr. Colvin had provided a splendid collation: cold roast chicken and baked ham, with bread and butter and dishes of asparagus, plum cake and fruit pies, and best of all, enormous bowls of strawberries and cream. There was lemonade or white wine for his guests to drink, according to their ages. When the cloth was laid on the grass they

111

all assembled for the feast. It was not a very conversational meal. Everyone was too busy eating.

Afterwards Mr. Colvin said they were all going to play French and English; he would captain one side and Mr. Lyman the other. Dick Lyman looked sulky, making it fairly plain that he considered himself too grand to play games with schoolgirls.

"Come along, my dear fellow," said his host. "It's no good pleading age and infirmity. If I can run about in the sun, you certainly can."

This made Dick look crosser than ever, but he was obliged to join in, and, to do him justice, he was soon pelting up and down the field, capturing more flags and more prisoners than anyone. Honor ran about too, as fast as her narrow skirt would let her. She was on the same side as Mr. Colvin, which was a relief, as she had no wish either to chase him or be chased by him. Lucy might have said something stupid when they got home.

By the time the game was over they were exhausted and everyone went to sit in the shade. Honor and Lucy found a comfortable bank under a tree. Colvin cast himself down between them. Not far off Martha was making a daisy chain for Evelina. Henrietta and Dick were laughing at some shared joke.

Colvin watched them for a time in silence. Honor thought he was about to make some comment, but his glance passed on to the lanky silhouette of Nancy fanning herself with her hat.

"How is young Kitty Fisher conducting herself these days?"

"She was never a pickpocket, Mr. Colvin," protested Lucy. "And she has become quite a reformed character, determined to make amends for all the trouble she has caused."

"I am glad to hear it. There was room for improvement. But is she not very stupid? I got the idea from Sally that she was a dunce."

"She isn't stupid," said Honor. "Her writing and spelling are bad because she has never been properly taught, bundled about from school to school and always in hot water. We have found that she reads very well and takes in what she reads. I have been lending her Scott's narrative poems."

"It is such a blessing that she can enjoy reading," said Lucy. "She is not happy at home, poor child, and a taste for literature, a doorway to other worlds, is such a great solace. I have often found it so."

"That is as good a reason as any for teaching girls to read," said Colvin.

Honor was annoyed by what she took to be a note of mockery and scepticism in his voice.

She said, "I expect you think one needs a reason—an excuse, in fact—for teaching girls anything that requires them to use their brains."

"I believe there are as many slow-witted girls in the world as slow-witted boys, and a formal education is not likely to achieve much for either. So you will have to work out which side that puts me on in your revolutionary war."

Honor bit her lip. She swore to herself that she was not going to lose her temper.

"How Irish you look," said her tormentor.

Lucy said hastily that they must think of starting for home.

Colvin rose at once and held out a hand to help her. When he turned to Honor, she had already scrambled to her feet, as though to demonstrate her independence.

"I meant it as a compliment," he told her softly. "Please don't be angry."

She felt ashamed of her ungraciousness, saying, "How could I be angry, when you have given us such a happy day!"

It had been a happy day, as the girls' faces showed when they gathered round the carriages, straw hats slung back over their shoulders and hanging by the strings, hair tumbled and noses peeling from the sun. There were grass stains on their light dresses and scratches on their arms, they were weary but content.

Lying in bed that night Honor could still see the green valley printed on her closed eyelids, still feel the trundling movement of the carriage wheels and the sensation of running over the short grass. I nearly spoiled it all, she thought, for myself at least, by quarreling with Marcus Colvin. Why?

A year ago it would not have troubled her to hear a man speak slightingly of education or reading. Although she had always read a great deal herself, she had known and liked plenty of men and women who hardly ever opened a book, unless it might be a Gothic novel. Since she started sharing a house with Lucy and trying to inspire these impressionable young girls, she had begun to feel that the furniture of people's minds was one of the most important things about them, more important than good looks or breeding. There was something disappointing in a clever, capable man who apparently cared so little for learning. Why she should mind so much, Honor did not need to inquire. Lucy was right. She did think too much about Marcus Colvin.

"Do play another tune, Hen," said Martha.

They were in the small upstairs schoolroom looking across to Oxford Row, a friendly room much used by the older girls. The walls were decorated with their lively portrait sketches and historical scenes, lovingly mounted and hanging not quite straight. There were pressed flowers drying under heavy books on every available piece of furniture. Henrietta was at the pianoforte. She was supposed to be practicing but had fallen into a daydream. She let her fingers run across the keyboard and a sequence of notes trickled lazily away into silence. Nancy was at the table, leaning on her elbows, and reading *The Lady of the Lake*. Martha was making a new dress for Marianne's doll. Honor had given her what she called her ragbag to choose from.

"Miss Clare must have had some beautiful clothes," she said, sorting through scraps of gauze and satin and velvet. "Look at this emerald green, how it must have suited her. Do you think her father lost all his money?"

"No," said Henrietta, "but when he died it had to go to a distant cousin because there was an entail. Miss Fielder told me."

"Poor Miss Clare." Martha selected a minute scrap of pink silk and started to make a sash. She was very neat fingered. "I suppose the cousin wasn't as agreeable as yours."

"Who? Oh, you mean Dick. Well, as a matter of fact, he isn't my cousin. I can't think how Miss Fielder and Miss Clare got hold of the idea that he was."

Martha stared at her. "Then who is he?"

"He's Mrs. Porcheston's godson. She is the lady whose family I was living with in Sussex. He— I—that is to say, we are very particular friends, though not related. I was going to explain to Miss Clare, only Dick said there was no need, and perhaps she might not let him come to the house so often. There can be nothing wrong in letting them think we are cousins. It's not as though he was claiming to be my brother; that would be different."

"Why?" asked the unworldly Martha. Then she grasped the point, adding quickly, "I expect you like to have a visit from a relation, even a pretend one."

"Yes. You know how dull it is to have hardly any family. There is only Grandpapa, and he is not even in England."

"My sisters and I have no one in England either."

"You don't know how lucky you are," broke in Nancy, looking up from Sir Walter Scott. "I wish my family was dead or in India. Then I could invent stories about how much they loved me, which I can never do while they are cross and disapproving at home."

"Don't say such things! How can you be so cruel?" cried Martha.

She burst into tears and ran out of the room, scattering the contents of the ragbag like a shower of bright petals behind her.

"Nancy, that was horrid of you," said Henrietta.

"I don't see what I said to send her into the vapors."

Nancy was genuinely puzzled. Since her fright in the haberdasher's shop, and the discovery that there was someone who really cared what became of her, she had tried to be more like ordinary people and to make friends, and she had found this easier than she had expected. In her rebellious days she had always been able to attract a following of children younger than herself. Now she found it possible to get along quite happily with the two older girls. In spite of this it was difficult, after years of ignoring the uses of tact and reserve, to recognize when these were necessary.

"I never said Martha's parents wanted to go off and leave her," she pointed out. "I don't suppose they wanted to go to India, any more than yours wanted to be drowned—Oh Lord! I suppose I shouldn't have said that either. I'm sorry."

"It doesn't signify. I can think about that quite calmly now. Martha hasn't got used to the idea yet of her parents going away. And I think there is something else. She sometimes looks so anxious."

Martha had taken refuge in her bedroom, flinging herself on the bed with her mouth pressed against the quilt to smother the sound of her crying. Nancy had suggested that if your parents were far enough away, you could go on thinking they loved you, but Martha's own experience was very different. Since she and her sisters had been left in Bath, she had slowly become obsessed with the idea that their father and mother had abandoned them.

"They wouldn't! They wouldn't!" she sobbed, knowing all the time that Papa could be driven to the most outrageous lengths when he was In Difficulties—the phrase always used in the Marlow family to describe the lowest ebb of Mr. Marlow's finances. And Mama would do anything Papa asked her.

It was wicked to suspect such a dreadful thing but Martha could not help it. All her life they had been running away from Papa's debts and this time the crisis had been worse than ever before. Mama had explained to her that some of his friends had promised to help him leave the country and take up a post in India. It was the only help they would now give him; they were tired of handing over money that usually went on play. Mama had also said that one of these kind friends was going to act as the children's guardian while they were at school, but she had not given his name or address to Miss Clare, no inquiry about them had come from London, and Martha was afraid that this unnamed guardian did not really exist.

She knew her parents had told Miss Clare at least one lie. They had spoken of their disappointment at another Bath school, saying it would not do because there had been vacancies for only two of the three girls. Martha knew this was not true. Arrangements with this other school had been made by letter and they were all three expected, but then there had been some kind of argument about the fees, and the Marlows had been obliged to retreat in discomfort, Mama looking quite ill with worry. That was when they had wandered into one of the circulating libraries, not knowing what to do next, and Papa had picked up a printed card about the school in Belmont. Here they had been accepted at once, a fact which had made Martha feel slightly uneasy.

She had no one she could confide in. To begin with she and Margaret had shared their misery at being left alone in England. But Margaret was only eleven; safe within the solid walls of the

118

school, busy all day in the regular variety of work and play, she had forgotten their original doubts. She and seven-year-old Marianne had missed their mother sporadically but now felt perfectly secure.

Martha got off the bed and went to bathe her eyes with cold water from the jug. She did not want either Miss Clare or Miss Fielder to know she had been crying. Kind as they were, she could not discuss her fears with them, because of the nagging of one unanswered question: if the other school had refused to take them, how had Miss Clare been able to do so? Martha could not face the shame of discovering that Papa had somehow cheated her over the fees.

She heard the sound of a bell ringing, of feet scampering on the stairs. The play hour was over; she must go down to an arithmetic lesson. She hated arithmetic, her sums never came out right. (She sometimes wondered if Papa suffered from the same disability.) By the end of the morning she had a good excuse for looking glum.

"I am afraid you will have to do this page again," said Miss Fielder with a sigh. "Don't be too despondent, my dear child. Miss Clare is taking you to the theater this evening, to see *Julius Caesar.*"

Martha immediately thought, I shall see *him*, and began to feel happier.

He was an actor called Samuel Harris, one of the company that spent most of their lives on the road between Bath and Bristol, performing in both cities. Martha had fallen violently in love with him. She had been to the theater a good deal lately. Miss Clare had promised Mrs. Porcheston that Henrietta should go whenever a suitable play

119

was being given. This meant taking a box, so two of the other girls were always included in the treat, generally Martha and Nancy, the nearest to Henrietta in age.

Martha had been able to worship her idol as Orlando and Captain Absolute. As she got ready this evening, putting on the muslin dress that Henrietta had lent her, she wondered what part he would play tonight.

"Not Caesar, I hope," she said to Margaret. "I couldn't bear to have him murdered less than half-way through."

"Perhaps he'll be Mark Antony."

But when they reached the Theater Royal it turned out that Mr. Harris had the long and sympathetic part of Brutus. Martha forgot all her own troubles, leaned eagerly on the edge of the box, and hardly drew breath until the interval. When the curtain fell, she remained in a trance, gazing dully around her at the horseshoe tiers of lights and faces rising up to the roof of the theater, the people so much less real to her than the actors had been on the stage. . . .

Of course Henrietta and Nancy knew all about Martha's passion for Samuel Harris and teased her about him in a good-natured way which she did not resent. They were not laughing at the unrequited love of Martha Marlow, fourteen and rather plain, for a dashing actor. Martha knew it was all a kind of game. They belonged to such different worlds, they were never likely to meet, so she could proudly indulge in all the pangs of a heroine and bask in the interest of her friends.

They were out for a walk by the river a few days later, when Nancy said, "Look! There's Sam Harris."

Martha jumped. "Where? Oh Nancy, you are a wretch—I wish you wouldn't play such tricks."

"No, I'm serious. Coming towards us, don't you see?"

They were strolling along the bank of the Avon just below the Paragon, some way behind Miss Fielder, who had one of the younger girls hanging on each arm and was telling them the story of Prince Bladud and the pigs bathing in the hot spring. Approaching them from the direction of Walcot Parade was a pensive figure with an open book in his hand—Mr. Samuel Harris, perhaps learning his lines for a new part. He was not quite so young, tall and debonair as he appeared on the stage, but striking enough in an actorish way. Martha, blinded by love, stood still and gaped.

"Now's your chance to meet him," said Nancy. "Can't you drop your handkerchief? Or swoon?"

"Or fall in the river," suggested Henrietta. "He would be obliged to fish you out."

By this time Mr. Harris had passed Miss Fielder and the little girls; he was drawing nearer to the heroine and her confidantes. Martha was puce with emotion, Henrietta and Nancy struggling to suppress their giggles. He stepped aside to avoid them but without raising his head or looking their way.

"I call that very ungallant." Nancy scowled at his retreating back.

"I said she ought to have fallen in the river."

"How could I?" protested Martha, taking this quite seriously.

"Easily, my dear. You had simply to step rather close to the edge whilst admiring the prospect. Such a pretty scene."

Henrietta performed this pantomime, gazing

121

sentimentally into the middle distance and failing to notice a patch of ground where the bank had crumbled away. Her foot slipped, she lost her balance and, greatly to her own astonishment, she actually did fall into the river.

She gave a loud shriek, more from surprise than fright, for though the water was not deep just there, it was very cold. She caught at an overhanging branch, it broke in her hand and she sat down. Miss Fielder, turning round, saw her in a little whirlpool of splashes. Horrified, she ran on to the grass verge, colliding with Martha.

Nancy was about to pull Henrietta out when she caught sight of Mr. Harris, hesitating a few yards from them, and thought she might as well put him to the test.

"Aren't you going to save her?" she demanded.

Poor Mr. Harris looked reluctantly at his smart coat and pantaloons. Like all actors, he was expected to dress well though chronically underpaid. However, he could hardly walk away and leave the young woman floundering in the water. There was no other man in sight.

Stoically he waded into the river. Henrietta grasped his arm and clung to him for a moment while she recovered her footing. As she did so he was astounded by the little face that smiled at him through the cascade of sparkling water that dripped from her dark red hair. He had hardly noticed the impact of the cold river, but this vision took his breath away.

As they stumbled on to dry ground, she was thanking him and he was hoping solicitously that she had not been too much alarmed.

"No, not at all, but I am most dreadfully wet. And you are too. I am so sorry."

122

She shook herself like a spaniel, which made Miss Fielder and Nancy wet as well. She could not catch Nancy's eye without wanting to laugh. And there was Martha, gazing at Handsome Harris with a perfectly besotted expression, it was all too ludicrous.

Henrietta thanked Mr. Harris again, Miss Fielder thanked him with equal enthusiasm, and they started for home. Henrietta's dress clung round her legs in a clammy and uncomfortable way that was positively indecent. She left a trail of water behind her, like a mermaid, and created quite a sensation.

"I can't understand how you came to fall in," said Miss Fielder, hurrying so that Henrietta should not catch cold.

Miss Clare could not understand it either, when they all burst in on her, damp and excited.

"What on earth were you thinking of, Henrietta? Rescued by whom? I wish you would not all talk at once. Who is Sam Harris? Oh, the actor.... How very odd, what was he doing there?"

She did not seem much impressed by a description of his noble conduct (supplied by Nancy) and said that Henrietta had better have a mustard bath.

About an hour later Martha was looking out of the window of the first floor schoolroom when she had a piece of amazing good luck. She was there at exactly the right moment to see Mr. Harris cross the Lansdown Road, vanish under the cliff-like projection of the high pavement as he climbed the steps, and reappear just outside their house.

She shot out on to the landing and was hanging over the bannisters when Pinker opened the front door.

A melodious voice, deep and thrilling as organ music, said: "I came to inquire after the young lady who had the accident. I hope she has suffered no ill effects?"

Before Pinker could answer, Miss Clare came out of the parlor, so he said the same thing again to her.

"She seems none the worse," said Miss Clare cheerfully, "but I must thank you for coming to her assistance so promptly. It was extremely kind of you, though I gather she was in no particular danger. I hope you did not get too cold and wet yourself? You cannot run risks with your voice."

Mr. Harris said he had an excellent constitution, he had only been anxious about the young lady, so white a complexion and such a slight build—he was afraid she might be delicate.

Once again Miss Clare reassured him, but though she was patient and polite and suitably grateful, she did not hold out any hope of his meeting Henrietta, did not even tell him her name. Eventually he made another speech and went away.

Miss Clare looked up and saw Martha at the top of the stairs.

"What are you doing there?"

"Nothing, Miss Clare."

"Wasting your time, my dear. The proper place for gazing at actors is a theater; in any other setting they are apt to disappoint one. By the way, how did Mr. Harris know where to find Henrietta? Have you any idea?"

"I—I think someone mentioned Belmont. He wanted to know whether we had far to go, whether he should try to find us a carriage. He was so kind."

"I am sure he was," said Miss Clare, smiling. "Now you had better go back to the schoolroom."

Martha sank into a mood of deep dejection. Not that she had been in the least disappointed by Mr. Harris, she only wished she had fallen in the river. What a fool she had been, to miss such an opportunity. Not that it would have made any difference. If he had rescued her instead of beautiful Henrietta, she did not think he would have come here afterwards to inquire about her. This made her feel very low and she began once again to wonder about her parents.

PART FIVE

Aspects of Love

Seeing *Julius Caesar* had awakened an interest in Roman history, classical architecture and so forth. Honor took some of the girls to sketch the famous Crescent. They chose a vantage point at the top of Crescent Fields, gazed up at the glorious arc of pale stone, and tried inadequately to put down on paper the receding perspective of Ionic pillars. Honor was moving from one artist to another, offering advice and pointing out that shadows all fell in the same direction, when she saw Marcus Colvin emerge from one of the houses and pause on the pavement. Then he came through a small gate in the railings, crossed the half-moon terrace of grass, and jumped down the ha-ha to join them.

"What an industrious party," he said. "May I look?"

His daughter was not among the sketchers, but of course he knew all the other girls quite well by now, and they showed him their work, with protests that it was not very good, which he could see for himself.

"Buildings are much harder than trees," observed Nancy. "The Crescent is designed after the Roman fashion, Mr. Colvin, did you know? Or perhaps it is Greek. Miss Clare did tell us which, only I forget."

"Get on with your drawing, Nancy," said Honor, "and don't chatter. Mr. Colvin is not interested in the Greeks."

"Now I wonder what gave you that idea," murmured Mr. Colvin.

Honor moved a little apart, as though studying the scene with great thoroughness. The geometric planes of reflected light made her eyes swim.

When he followed her, she said, "I wish you would not try to undermine my authority by laughing at me."

"I beg your pardon, Portia. That was the last thing I intended."

"Why do you call me that?" she asked. Suspiciously, for it struck her that Portia had been rather an overbearing female, dressing up as a man and arguing points of law.

"The Lady of Belmont," said Marcus Colvin blandly.

"Oh. I see." She was disarmed.

"I have just taken rooms in the Crescent," he informed her. "I shall move in this afternoon. I'm sick of living in a hotel. As I mean to stay in Bath for the present, I shall do better here. By the way, I see there is a Gala Night in Sydney Gardens this week; may I take you to it? I have a passion for fireworks which I hope you share."

"Of course I cannot go with you to Sydney Gardens! Though it is extremely kind of you to ask me."

"Why can't you?"

She did not know what to say. The simple answer was that an unmarried woman of her age could not spend an evening at a place of public entertainment, unchaperoned, with a man who was not related to her. Under those rules he had no right to ask her. Yet by transforming herself from a young lady into a schoolmistress, she supposed she had renounced her youth; she was now one of those dull, worthy females who could make themselves useful by chaperoning others. Only in that case, why should he want to ask her?

She was struggling with this dilemma, when he said, "Some old friends of mine, Mr. and Mrs. Barry have just arrived in Bath and I have asked them to meet you. They have five daughters, it is a great affliction."

"I'm sure it must be. Though I don't quite see—"

"Wouldn't you like five new boarders? Not all at once; the youngest Miss Barry is not quite two years old, but that is the way to build up a connection; younger sisters coming along as the elders leave. Don't you agree?"

"You are amusing yourself, Mr. Colvin. I can hardly hope that you will recommend our school to any of your friends. I am not such a simpleton."

To her surprise, this shot went home. He flushed under the sunburn, losing his usual poise.

"My dear girl, are you still angry with me for the way I behaved when we first met? You must know I have entirely changed my opinion. Surely you realized that I no longer have any intention of removing Sally, and that should convince you if nothing else does."

Honor was so pleased that she found herself accepting his invitation almost without thinking it over.

On her way back to the school she admitted defeat—privately, to herself if to no one else: she was in love. What it was about that infuriating man she did not know, only that he had maneuvered his way through her defences. And she did not care. He was staying on in Bath, he was leaving Sally at the school, he was taking her to Sydney Gardens. Exhilarated, she marched along Brock Street and across the Circus with an inelegant countrywoman's stride, her little flock trotting behind her.

And then she was brought up with a new shock as soon as she reached Belmont.

She was seized on by Lucy.

"Honor, I must talk to you. I have had a letter from Edward."

Edward was her brother, a curate in Yorkshire. She looked so agitated that Honor said, "I hope it is not bad news. Your brother is not ill?"

"Oh no! It has nothing to do with Edward himself. It is about Mr. Colvin."

Honor had a sudden sensation of cold round the heart and felt it sink through her whole body. She had temporarily forgotten her old distrust of him. For weeks she had been wanting to hear something that could be held against him. Now she dreaded anything of the kind. What disturbing rumor could have reached a remote parish in Yorkshire? She waited.

Lucy unfolded her brother's letter and began to read:

... I was most interested to learn that one of your charges is a daughter of Marcus Colvin. You do not seem to have realized when you wrote, though by now perhaps you are aware, that he is justly celebrated as the foremost living translator of Homer. His version of the *Iliad* . . .

"Good God!" exclaimed Honor, sitting down abruptly and gaping at Lucy in sheer disbelief. "Homer? Nonsense, it can't be the same man."

"I think it must be. Listen: 'His version of the *Iliad* received great praise when it came out four years ago, even *The Quarterly Review* could find few bones to pick. I was lucky enough to borrow a copy and found it first-rate. Since then Mr. Colvin has served as an attaché on a mission we sent to the Sublime Porte; it is generally believed that he went there in order to explore various sites of antiquity, and while there he offended the Turks by championing the cause of Greek independence, so that our people were obliged to disown him, officially at least. He is supposed to have had many adventures and we must hope that these will help to animate his forthcoming translation of the *Odyssey.* . . .' So I think it is undoubtedly our Mr. Colvin, don't you?"

Honor began to see clearly for the first time through many misunderstandings and ambiguities, but was able to focus only on the last of them.

"I've just told Nancy that he didn't care about the Greeks."

"Well, she is not likely to pass it on."

"He was there. He heard me and he was laughing—good heavens, now I see why! What an ignoramus he must think me! And it is so unjust: why did he lead us on to think that he despised education and learning? I suppose it is the usual prejudice—educated women are what he despises."

"No," said Lucy firmly. "I am afraid the prejudice was on your side. Ever since I read Edward's letter, I have been piecing together what Mr. Colvin told us at the picnic: he considers there are as many stupid girls in the world as stupid boys, and such children don't benefit from a formal education. It is a little arrogant, but he is probably right, and I dare say such a very clever man is frequently irked by having his enthusiasms dampened by uncomprehending ignorance. Perhaps this accounts for the offhand, ironic manner which misled us."

Honor had the grace to recognize that this was very likely true. She had been prejudiced against him, chiefly on account of that dreadful coat. She began to feel awkward and stupid, wondering how she was to behave at their next meeting. The evening in Sydney Gardens now loomed ahead with a prospect of appalling awkwardness. She told herself that she would have cried off, but for the inducement of meeting the couple with all those little girls. She felt it was her duty not to let such an opportunity slip, as she explained to Lucy, but she began to feel self-conscious about the whole scheme; no one else in the school was to know where she was going. The expedition sounded so frivolous, she half hoped it would be canceled. Perhaps it would rain.

The evening turned out warm and clear. Mr. Colvin came to fetch her. Mr. and Mrs. Barry were already in the carriage, so there was no private conversation on the drive to Bathwick. The Barrys were a pleasant, unaffected couple who seemed to admire her enterprise in starting a school, and were not in the least condescending.

The Sydney Hotel stood at the far end of Great

Pulteney Street, porticoed and set apart like a little palace, with Sydney Gardens spreading out from it on three sides. Beyond the hotel there was a semicircle of refreshment boxes, with a bar in the center and a raised orchestra where a string band was already playing the music of Rossini and other popular composers. It was one of the four annual Galas and the place was crowded with well-to-do people, for the tickets were expensive. Mr. Colvin's party strolled about, admiring the scene. The Gardens had been designed nearly forty years ago to emulate Vauxhall, but nowadays there was rather less emphasis on the artificial cascade made by turning a painted roller, and similar illusions. There was a real waterfall embowered in a romantic grove of trees, a bowling green and a maze, planted in 1805, which was now high enough for people to lose themselves, so that a man had to be kept on duty to guide them out.

At first Mr. Barry took charge of Honor and kept her amused. Then they went back to their reserved box and had a cold supper. It was still too light for the fireworks.

"How hot it is," said Mrs. Barry, fanning herself. "I think I shall stay here and watch the world go by, but don't let me prevent you from exploring."

She smiled at Mr. Colvin, who said to Honor, "Shall we go and look at the canal?"

The Kennet and Avon Canal had been dug straight through Sydney Gardens, to the fury of the proprietor, until he realized that this narrow strip of water added a new element of beauty to his grassy slopes and deeply shadowed trees. Two cast iron bridges in the Chinese manner had been thrown across the canal, and presently Honor and

Marcus Colvin were standing on one of these, gazing into the glassy stillness below.

"You are very silent," he said. "Is anything the matter?"

She took a long breath. "Can you not guess, Mr. Colvin? I have found you out at last."

"The devil you have!" He sounded so disconcerted that she might really have wondered whether he had some nefarious secret after all.

"Why didn't you tell us you were a famous classical scholar?"

"Well, I am a scholar of sorts, but it is not a thing one goes around boasting of to people who may not wish to hear."

"Yes," she acknowledged that. "It was a stupid question, and I have been very stupid all along."

"We got off on the wrong foot, didn't we? From the very first day."

She thought of it now, from his point of view: arriving at the school, asking for his daughter and finding that she was playing truant somewhere in the city.

"I'm afraid that was my fault too," she said.

"Not entirely. I was in a mood to make difficulties."

He paused for a moment, staring along the canal to the arch of light, perfectly mirrored to form a full moon, under the next bridge. A noisy party passed them and went laughing up the slope.

He said, "I think you must be aware that my marriage was unhappy. Sarah's ideas and mine differed on every subject—not that she had a single idea in her head, poor girl, beyond the secondhand beliefs and conventions that had been planted there by her dull family. I'm afraid I was

133

very unkind to her; no need to go into that. The fact is, we didn't suit. I began my translation of the *Iliad* to occupy my time with something better than quarreling. Soon after it was finished, Sarah left me, taking Sally with her...

"I hadn't the heart to separate such a young child from her mother, and it happened that I had just been offered the chance of accompanying our Ambassador to Turkey as a super numerary attaché, with the possibility of traveling all over Greece and Asia Minor. I was out there when Sarah died. My sister-in-law wrote assuring me that she would be responsible for Sally; I had a feeling I ought to go home, which I quieted by telling myself that a little girl of seven would be better and safer in a home she knew with her aunt; there was nothing useful I could do for her. By now I had got myself embroiled in the question of Greek independence."

"Do the Turks treat them very badly?"

"Abominably. And of all nations in the world, the inspirers of all our learning, practically the first Christians, should not be under the tyranny of such brutes! But I mustn't let my hobbyhorse run away with me. I caused so much trouble that the Ambassador had to hustle me out of the way before the Turks locked me up. Incidentally, my respectable sister-in-law has got it into her head that I must have committed some fearful crime, if not high treason. I expect she painted a pretty black picture of me?"

"To begin with, she just let us think Sally was an orphan."

He laughed, "So she did. I'd forgotten. She must have hoped I'd die of fever or get my throat cut. However, I escaped to Sicily and came home in the end, on a British man-of-war, and even then I had another adventure, for we nearly went down in a storm less than fifty miles off the coast of Cornwall. When I finally landed at Plymouth, I went to see a cousin of my wife's, a good-natured woman married to a naval officer, quite unlike most of the Butley tribe. She gave me the news that Maria Butley had found herself a husband at last and my little Sally had been packed off to a Bath boarding school. I was furious. After all that talk of regarding her beloved Sarah's child as a sacred trust, she couldn't be rid of her quick enough. And I felt guilty too; Sally was my daughter and I'd been just as selfish. So I came straight to Bath and vented my guilt and resentment on you."

"Yes, I understand now," said Honor. "No wonder you were bitter. Especially when you discovered what sort of a school it was that Sally had been sent to. Of course you wanted to snatch her away immediately. Indeed, I am astonished that you have been able to overcome your first bad impression. Do you really want to leave her with us now?"

"You must know I do," he replied. "Anything precious of mine I would entrust to you, surely you must realize by now?"

There was a curious, rough note of emotion in his voice she had not heard before. He laid his hand over hers on the rail of the bridge, pressing so hard that the metallic edge seemed to bite into her palm, and from his touch she felt a current of excitement and expectancy tingle through her body.

"Dear Portia, I have no right to—there is something I ought to tell you. To explain."

"Yes?"

He changed his mind apparently, for he removed his hand, and she heard him mutter something about leaving well alone.

And after that, in a tone of cool detachment, "There is something insidiously dangerous about a garden at dusk. One is led into the most hare-brained follies."

Honor did not ask what he meant. Being no longer a romantic innocent of seventeen, she was pretty sure she knew. Marcus would not make love to a woman of her kind unless he could offer her marriage, and he could not afford to marry a woman who had hardly any money of her own to contribute. Well, what else had she imagined? It was childish to feel ill-used or disappointed.

She moved slightly, avoiding his eye, looking beyond him, up the final stretch of the Gardens, and saw a girl step out onto the lawn just below the little round temple at the top. A girl in a green dress with a cloud of dark red hair.

"Henrietta!" exclaimed Honor.

"What?" Colvin was at a loss.

"Henrietta—I saw her. Over there in front of the rotunda."

He swung round but the girl in green had vanished between the trees.

"I must go after her," said Honor. "The little wretch—she's no business to be here. Who can have persuaded her to come?"

"Are you sure it was Henrietta? The light is beginning to fail...."

"I saw her quite plainly and she saw me. I know it was her."

While they were talking, another argument

136

was taking place in whispers close to the wall that ran behind the rotunda.

"Miss Clare is standing on the bridge with Mr. Colvin, and she saw me. Oh Dick, whatever are we to do?"

Dick Lyman swore. "Are you certain she recognized you?"

"Of course she did. She'll write and tell the Porchestons that I was meeting you and they'll be so angry. I shall never be allowed to see you again."

Dick caught her by the wrist.

"Keep your head down and run."

He led her away from the rotunda where they were in danger of being cornered. When he felt comfortably hidden among the bushes he stopped, and they stood still, panting. They could dodge about here indefinitely in the increasing dusk, rejoin the crowds in the lower part of the Gardens perhaps, and slip out unseen. He could take Henrietta home. But they both knew this would not save them from disaster, for how was Henrietta to get back into the school? She had left a window open in the basement before coming out to meet him. Now, most likely, Miss Clare would get back before she did, and would be waiting for her when she crept in.

"I tell you what," said Dick. "She may have seen you but she didn't see me. We'll have to pretend you came here to meet someone else. That actor fellow—Harris, he jumped into the river for you, didn't he? He'll do."

Henrietta gasped. "I couldn't tell such a story— you must be mad. I don't even know Mr. Harris and I certainly wouldn't have made an assignation with him."

"Listen, Hen," said Dick fiercely. "If you say
137

you were with Harris, you'll get off with a scolding but I shall still be able to come and visit you. If you tell them the truth, I shall never see you again, and that will be the end of our engagement."

Henrietta stopped protesting. She was always ready to do what Dick told her, and the fear of losing him outweighed every other consideration.

Dick stepped out into the open and hurried across the grass with an expression of relief.

"Miss Clare! Thank God I have found you—I suppose you have come to look for my cousin? Did you know she was here with Sam Harris?"

"With Harris?" repeated Honor in dismay. "Good God, it is worse than I thought."

She and Marcus Colvin had spent the last few minutes stalking a couple in the bushes who turned out to be complete strangers. It was a situation worthy of a Drury Lane farce and would have amused her if she hadn't been so anxious. She listened impatiently as Dick described how he had been at the Gala with a party of friends, and catching sight of Henrietta and her escort, had hardly been able to believe his eyes.

"But where are they now? I must go to her at once."

"Harris beat a retreat directly I spoke to them. Didn't want any trouble with the young lady's family. Henrietta is waiting over there. Please don't be too severe with her, Miss Clare. I think she only did it for a lark, without considering what a scrape she might get into."

"She will have plenty of time to think about it now. Could you find us a carriage, Mr. Colvin? And make my excuses to Mr. and Mrs. Barry."

"Of course."

The pleasure of the evening was over for Honor; in any case it had ended abruptly on the bridge, with Marcus's return to common sense. As Dick led forward the pale and reluctant Henrietta, the fireworks began to fizzle and pop, and the first set piece blazed into view: two hearts entwined against a darkening sky.

(2)

Henrietta sat in a barely furnished room on the second floor, hemming a pillowcase and sniffing as she sewed. She was banished to this bleak prison for every hour that she was not actually doing lessons, with none of her possessions around her, no books, nothing but a basket of plain sewing. This was to be her fate for the rest of the week.

She had accepted the punishment without really caring, she felt too frightened and guilty. Not about her love for Dick, their secret engagement, or the adventure in Sydney Gardens. Her infatuation had blunted her moral sensibilities, she was afraid they would be found out and separated—which was why she had gone along with the pretence that she had been meeting Mr. Harris. Miss Clare had talked to her very seriously about the false glamor of the stage and the stupidity of becoming besotted with a middle-aged actor. She had threatened to report the whole matter to Mrs. Porcheston.

This had really alarmed Henrietta, for Dick was bound to feature in the story and the Porchestons knew all about her attachment to Dick, which Miss Clare obviously did not. Mrs. Porcheston would guess the truth, and would be even angrier than she had been when the Rector had caught them kissing in the drawing room at Brauncing.

Henrietta had taken refuge in tears, and a wicked idea had come into her head.

"Please, please don't tell them," she had begged, and her sobs were perfectly genuine. "I promise you on my solemn word of honor that I will never see or communicate with Mr. Harris again. Indeed I don't want to see him, it would be too humiliating."

And Miss Clare had believed her, she was not going to give Henrietta away to the Porchestons. Of course the solemn promise would be kept, Henrietta had not the smallest desire to meet the inoffensive and maligned Mr. Samuel Harris. This was what made her feel so guilty, she was deceiving Miss Clare, the promise had never been anything but an empty sham. She was a religious girl, and though she had not actually committed perjury or taken the Lord's name in vain, she felt as though she had done something just as bad. If only she could escape from this tangle of secrecy and deceit.

Alice, the fat housemaid, put her head round the door and said with a conspiratorial wink, "A visitor to see you, miss."

"A visitor? Who—oh, Dick!"

She flung herself into his arms.

"Easy on," he said, patting her and kissing her wet eyelids. "My poor little love, what a state you're in. Have they been very unkind to you?"

"No more than I deserved, I suppose. Only I have felt dreadfully low, not knowing when I should see you. How did you get in?"

"I waited until I saw the Beauteous Clare taking the girls for some health-giving exercise. I

140

gather old Fielder is ministering to Evelina who seems to have Gone Off in one of her fits and fallen over the doorstep."

Henrietta giggled. "Poor Evelina, she is unlucky."

Dick perched on the edge of the table and turned his coinlike profile towards her. His dark hair was carefully ruffled, his dark eyes bright and keen; he looked a wonderfully Byronic hero.

"I think we had better start for Scotland as soon as possible."

Henrietta gazed at him with a mixture of hope and dread. He had convinced her that an elopement would provide their only chance of getting married before she came of age, and that would not be for nearly six years. She was an heiress and her grandfather had set his heart on marrying her to an heir, the son of someone who also had a great deal of money and property and perhaps a title as well. It seemed such a waste, two rich people marrying each other. When Dick would make her the best possible husband, and the income he hadn't got was the one thing she would never need. She had already agreed that they would have to go to Scotland.

"I hate the thought of distressing Grandpapa, but it's his own fault."

"He'll come round once we are married. I suppose you are sure of that, Hen?"

She was quite sure. She was the last Delahaye, he would never cast her off. Or try to undo the marriage, because once she had lived with Dick as his wife, it would cause too great a scandal. And when he actually consented to meet Dick, of course, he would realize how sensible she had been and all would be forgiven.

"Today's Tuesday," said Dick. "I'll need to plan our campaign, so we'll set out on Thursday. We'd better go up through Gloucestershire and strike eastwards on to the Great North Road somewhere in the Midlands."

"Grandpapa has a house in Gloucestershire," said Henrietta helpfully. "Couldn't we stay there on the way?"

"Don't be childish, Hen," he said crushingly. "Surely you realize that we shall be traveling as fast as we can, so as to get across the border before anyone catches up with us. We can't waste time fooling around in Gloucestershire. And that reminds me, you had better keep up the charade about Harris, pretend he's the man you're running off with."

"Oh no, Dick! Must I?" she wailed. "I do so dislike telling lies and it seems dreadful to pretend I want to marry anyone except you. Why do I have to?"

"Because it may cause confusion and hold up the pursuit. Even if your Miss Clare doesn't come dashing after us (and I wouldn't put it past her), she will send an express to Sussex and we shall have John Porcheston leading the hunt. Even with a good start, we must make the most of every advantage we can get."

The fear of being overtaken on the road conquered all her scruples.

"When do you want to start?" she asked. She had a vague impression that elopements usually took place by moonlight. "I don't think I can very easily get out of the house at night, now they are watching me. But I might manage in the early morning, before the maids get up."

"Yes, I thought of that. I'll have a post chaise
142

and four waiting at the bottom of Guinea Lane on Thursday morning just before six."

After he had kissed Henrietta goodbye and told her how much he loved her (something she seemed anxious to hear rather too frequently) Dick left her to her penitential sewing and went off in search of amusement. He bought a handsome pair of pistols that had taken his fancy in a gunsmith's shop. After all, one ought to be armed against highwaymen when eloping to Scotland with an heiress. He passed some time gossiping and reading the papers at a coffeehouse in the Organge Grove, and later dined on steak and claret at a slightly disreputable tavern, where he met one of the ladies of the town, whom he took back to his lodging.

He had done this fairly often during his stay in Bath. It was intolerably slow, hanging round a girls' school, making sheep's eyes at one of the parlor boarders, especially as he had promised his godmother that he would not "harm" Henrietta before they were married. He was not in love with her, would not have considered marrying her if he hadn't been so desperate for money. He found well brought up virgins decidedly tame; he much preferred his women luscious and experienced, like this self-styled Clarinda, with her breasts like ripe peaches bursting out of her low-cut dress of shiny red satin. Even her vulgarity was a stimulus.

He manhandled her towards the bed, remarking that they might as well get to work straight away.

"Not so fast, my lad," objected the lady. "I'm not one of your cheap nobodies huddling in a doorway.

I like to get acquainted with a gentleman over a glass of wine."

Scowling, Dick said he had no wine, but he fetched a bottle of brandy from the side table and two glasses. He would not have humored her impudence, only she had somehow made him seem mean.

"And a biscuit," said Clarinda. "If you have any. I dined early and I'm famished."

He was able to produce a few stale Bath Olivers.

The young woman took one and crumbled it between her fingers. They both raised their glasses and drank. It was the last thing Dick remembered that night.

He was woken eventually by a spasm of cramp in his left leg and discovered that he was very cold, he had a racking headache and the room was dark apart from a streak of light between the curtains, which puzzled him, for the window was on the wrong side of the room. He then realized that he was not in bed, but slumped in a chair. He remembered everything. The girl—what had happened? Surely he hadn't drunk himself insensible?

He staggered across the room and tugged back one of the curtains, letting in the bruised light of early dawn. He really did feel ill, much worse than he would have expected from the amount of claret and brandy he'd swallowed. As if he'd been drugged . . .

For the first time he noticed the chest of drawers. Last night the drawers had been closed, now they were all slightly open as though they had been searched. With a groan of disbelief he stumbled over to investigate. Not much had been taken; apparently Clarinda was not interested in his brushes, razors or shirts. But from the back of the drawer where he kept his neckcloths a leather purse had gone—the purse containing the gold and banknotes which Cecilia Porcheston had given him to finance the journey to Scotland.

Dick collapsed on the bed, feeling weak with shock. Presently he got himself a drink of water, though it was some while before he could think at all clearly, and then he wasted some minutes cursing that thieving harlot and imagining what he would do to her if he ever caught her.

Only he never would catch her. He knew enough of the world to realize that either she was unknown at the tavern where she had accosted him, or else she had accomplices there who would keep their mouths shut. And after such a good haul, she would not need to follow her profession for several days. In the meantime, what the devil was he to do about Henrietta?

Put off the elopement, while he wrote to his godmother and told her he'd been robbed? Naturally he would have to rearrange the circumstances a little. She would still be willing to help him, no doubt of that, he could twist her round his little finger, but it might take her some time to raise the second loan without that spoilsport of a parson finding out. Dick was not sure how she had done it before; sold some jewelry probably, and she might not have anything else she could sell. He could not afford to wait long for fresh funds, because he was nervous about Henrietta, who was having a very tiresome attack of conscience and would probably confess the whole truth to Miss Clare if she remained much longer in Belmont.

So what was he to do? It did just cross his mind that he might give up the whole idea of marrying Henrietta Delahaye, but he had got himself into the way of counting on their great future wealth, and life without it was too dreary to contemplate. All that money and an ignorant, obedient little girl who adored him and would do exactly what she was told: it would be madness to throw away such a prize.

What was that she had said about Grandpapa's house in Gloucestershire? She'd suggested staying there on their journey, as the place must be empty. Well, he would take her there, not in a chaise and four but in his curricle. He still had some money left, for luckily that bitch had not picked his pockets. Once they reached this house, wherever it was, no one would know where to look for them; in a way it would be safer than making the traditional dash for the border. And the chances were they would never need to go to Scotland at all, for little Hen was so much in love with him, he'd have her tumbling eagerly into his bed the first night they were together. And once she had become his mistress, that old grandfather of hers would be only too thankful to allow the marriage.

In spite of his headache, Dick began to feel a good deal more cheerful.

(3)

Four days after the Sydney Gardens episode, Honor was beginning to feel puzzled by Henrietta's continued nervousness and low spirits. She had behaved badly and had to be taught a lesson—if only to prevent her or anyone else in the school, especially Nancy, from thinking they could get away with such adventures. But the whole thing had been a silly prank, no harm had

146

come of it, so why did Henrietta still look so unhappy?

"You don't think she can possibly be in love with Harris, do you?" Honor asked Lucy. "It seems so unlikely. He is just the sort to inspire little Martha's schoolgirl adoration, but Henrietta is older and so much more mature; ready to take an interest in young men of her own station, rather than idolizing a middle-aged actor."

"I dare say Mr. Harris showed signs of idolizing her, which can be very flattering to a young girl. And then he took to his heels as soon as her cousin appeared. She must have felt the humiliation."

"Let's hope it will teach her not to be so silly."

While she talked and thought about Henrietta, Honor tried to stop thinking about herself and her own much more culpable silliness: falling in love at her age with a man whom she could not hope to marry. Marcus Colvin had gone to London, to see his publisher, so he said, though she suspected he was trying to avoid any more emotional encounters. Standing on the bridge in the soft evening light, he had felt the tug of desire as strongly as she had, she was convinced of that, and surely it was not conceited to think so? If he had simply wanted an amusing flirtation, he would have gone ahead. His sudden volte-face was a retreat from something more serious. He was a poor man, she imagined. He had married one heiress, but Sarah Butley's fortune would have been tied up and settled on Sally. In any case one could not respect a man who proposed to support his second wife on his first wife's money. Marcus had lost his diplomatic appointment because he had shown too much concern for the persecuted Greeks. His translation of Homer could hardly bring him much of an income, and he had no house of his own, just a furnished lodging. A man who could manage fairly comfortably on his own might be totally unable to provide for a wife and family. In which case, wouldn't he be wise to stay out of temptation?

Surely we can go on meeting as friends, she thought with a mixture of hope and desolation, checking stores in her basement larder. (Nearly out of sugar and tea again, how did everything go so quickly?) To talk and exchange ideas and spar a little; she had only just realized how much pleasure it had given her to know that Marcus might appear round any corner as she walked about Bath. Such pleasures would be better than nothing. Or did people always begin by thinking that, and end in disillusion, with their unfulfilled love turning sour?

She did not know the answer and was sick of her own self-questioning. A letter from Mrs. Bilting produced a distraction. "Corisande's mother is taking her away," she announced when she had read the first few lines.

"Oh dear, what a pity," said Lucy. "I hope she is not dissatisfied?"

"No, I don't think so. She says she is making new arrangements."

"What sort of new arrangements?"

Honor had by now turned over the page. "She is sending her to France to be educated in a convent."

"But that is dreadful! They will make her a Roman Catholic!"

"I expect they'll try. On the other hand, they may be better equipped than we are to alter her destiny." Honor looked with some amusement at her partner's shocked face. "Which would you rather—that Corisande became a nun or a courtesan?"

Lucy, the true daughter of an English parsonage, said it was no laughing matter.

Honor did not think either of these fates was going to overtake Corisande, who seemed exactly the kind of girl who was bound to make a prudent marriage. She greeted the news quite calmly and at once began to think about her packing. It was Tuesday, and her mother's housekeeper was coming to collect her the following day. Honor was sorry to lose her, but less sorry than she would have been to lose any of the others, even Evelina. In spite of her circumstances, which cried out for compassion, Corisande was the only girl in the school for whom Honor felt she could do practically nothing. She seemed so perfectly satisfied with her world as it was. Her friends Margaret and Sally were really distressed when she left next morning. Corisande embraced them with cool murmurings of affection and promised to write.

"I will tell you all about Paris, it is sure to be much more amusing than Bath, and I dare say Mama has friends there."

Honor thought the nuns were probably going to hear a good deal about French dukes.

That same evening Marcus Colvin returned to Bath and came round to call on them, though it was quite late and he must have known Sally would be in bed. Honor's spirits began to revive.

They had just made the tea, Lucy told him. He drank a cup and said how refreshing it was; Lucy muttered something incomprehensible about finding a recipe for boiled ham, and left the room.

149

Marcus had brought a parcel with him, which he now handed to Honor.

"I want to give you this."

It was a handsome leather-bound copy of his *Iliad*. She exclaimed with delight, and turning to the first page saw his name in print, also the august name of John Murray. She dipped a little further and read a few lines which at this moment she could hardly take in.

"How very kind of you to bring me such a present. Will you inscribe it for me?"

"If you wish."

He did not do so at once, though she was longing to see what he would put. Perhaps he had not made up his mind. They began to talk of other things.

"How have you all been going on while I was away? I hope Miss Henrietta has not been kicking up any more larks?"

"No, she still seems very subdued. We have lost a pupil, however: Corisande's mother has decided to send her to France."

"Yes, I know."

Honor was puzzled. "How can you possibly know?"

"I called on her in Hertford Street. You need not look so prim. Under the strange laws that govern our society, it is less improper for me to meet Antoinette Biiting than for Sally to associate with her daughter. We have been acquainted for years. She is not my mistress, I assure you."

"I don't care whether she is your mistress or not!" flashed Honor, actually believing that this was true. All other emotions had suddenly been swamped by the idea that he was trying to overrule and dominate her and the way she ran the
150

school. "I won't have you interfering in my affairs. That's what you've been doing, isn't it? I suppose you told that unfortunate woman that poor little Corisande wasn't fit to go to school with the children of respectable people—"

"I said nothing of the kind. I simply remarked how interesting it was that our daughters were schoolfellows; Antoinette became rather thoughtful and said she did not want the child's friendships to be a source of bitterness later on. The people she meets in France won't know or care about her circumstances in England. It won't affect them."

"They will force her to become a Roman Catholic," said Honor, using Lucy's argument.

"Does it matter? In any case, her mother is a Catholic already, if a lax one. She was born in France and brought over here as a child, during the Revolution."

"Oh." This temporarily floored Honor, who was unwise enough to say, "You probably think differences in religion are quite unimportant."

"I'm not a bigot. I believe all Christian churches have some share of the truth, and I fancy I know more about such things than you do."

"Of course you are bound to think that. Because you are a man and I am only a woman!"

"Don't talk such damned nonsense!" he almost shouted, losing his temper as thoroughly as she had. "Not because you are a woman—because I am ten years older than you, I have traveled more and read more, and above all, I have lived in a country where Christians are persecuted by Moslems. And while we are about it, I wish you would stop indulging your sense of grievance every time anyone dares to criticize you. I see what is going to happen, thanks to Mary Wolstonecraft and her imitators: no woman is ever going to be in the wrong again. No matter what disasters she brings about, no matter how rash or stupid she may have been, she will have the perfect defence. She cannot be held responsible because she is merely the innocent victim of male prejudice."

"I think you had better go," said Honor in what she hoped was a voice of cold disdain.

Marcus too had flushed, his eyes were hard and brilliant and he had that dangerous, catlike look she had disliked when they first met.

"You accused me of interfering. Perhaps you would like to reflect on this: if the Bilting child had remained here, the school would have been ruined as soon as the other parents realized whose daughter she was. I told you so weeks ago and you refused to listen. Not because you are a woman—many women would have seen the point quicker than a man—but because you are quixotic and pigheaded and careless of public opinion. Not fit to be allowed out without a nursemaid. Now I'd better go before I say something I might regret."

Lucy heard the front door slam. She was lurking in the empty schoolroom where she had gone so that Mr. Colvin and Honor could have a little time by themselves. She knew that he came to the school so often because he was strongly attracted to Honor, and she was fairly sure that Honor was in love with him or on the verge of it. Lucy had never been in love, it was not in her line, but she was not in the least jealous; she would be delighted to see Honor happily married—if only she was not haunted by the dreadful uncertainty of her own future. For if Honor married Mr. Colvin she would need the Belmont house, either to live in or to sell, the school would have to close, Lucy's brief independence would be over and she would be back where she was in February: eating up her small savings and looking for a post as a governess.

She was so absorbed in her own thoughts that the sound of the front door took her by surprise.

She picked up her candle and composed a smiling expression, ready to hear good news if they had reached that stage. Ready, at any rate, to encourage Honor's happiness and not be a wet blanket.

Honor was walking up and down the parlor in a rage.

"That detestable man—I never want to see him again!"

"Good gracious, what has he done now?"

Lucy was quite upset when she heard, and scrupulously suppressed a flicker of relief because Honor was obviously not on the point of marrying Mr. Colvin.

Honor lay staring into the darkness a good part of the night, still raging against Marcus. She would never forgive him, trying to lord it over her with his masculine superiority. And as for imagining herself into love with him—it had all been a mistake, of course, due to the fact that she hardly met any other men. Lucy had foreseen that. Schoolmistresses could not expect to have husbands, or children of their own. They were luckier than most unmarried women in having so much to occupy their minds and energies. And anyway, how could she have abandoned the school? Lucy depended on her.

Gradually, as she went over her quarrel with Marcus, she started to feel embarrassed by her own performance. What on earth had made her talk about Roman Catholics in that narrow, ignorant way she found so ridiculous in Lucy? Or champion the Biltings, mother and daughter, as though they were pathetic victims, when she knew they were nothing of the sort? It was all the fault of that hateful man, and as for his book, still lying on the table downstairs, neglected and unsigned, she would never read a word of it.

Being thoroughly overwrought she stayed awake until the early hours, and then fell into a kind of stupor from which she was aroused, just before eight o'clock, by Lucy shaking her.

"Do wake up, Honor: the most dreadful thing has happened. Henrietta has gone off with Mr. Harris!"

"Gone Off?" mumbled Honor, recognizing one well-worn phrase through the mists of sleep that still clouded her mind. "You mean Evelina. Henrietta doesn't have fits."

"No, not that sort of going off—I mean she has eloped. She has gone to Scotland with Mr. Harris."

"I don't believe you!" said Honor, becoming suddenly and painfully awake.

"She left a note behind. It was addressed to us both, so I opened it."

Honor took the single sheet of paper, the words wavered in front of her.

Dear Miss Clare and Miss Fielder,

I am sorry I deceived you about Sam Harris, it was very wrong of me. I am going to Scotland to be married. Do not be anxious for me as I am so happy and

I know Grandpapa will come round in the end. Please forgive me.

Henrietta

"Good God, I would not have thought it possible! And after she made me those solemn promises that she would never see him again. She volunteered to do so, the cunning little liar, I didn't even ask her."

"It quite destroys one's faith in human nàture. What are we to do now? Send at once to Mrs. Porcheston?"

"Yes, but that will take some time. I think I ought to go after them myself and try to bring them back." Honor jumped out of bed and started pulling on her clothes. "I'll get hold of Dick Lyman, I dare say he would come with me."

She left the house in ten minutes, begging Lucy to try and keep the news from the rest of the girls. It was probably too late. As she hurried through the hall she could hear Alice informing Pinker that they could have knocked her down with a feather.

Honor knew that Dick lodged in St. James's Parade with a Mrs. Green. It took a few inquiries to find the right house, but then there was a disappointment: the landlady informed her that he had driven out of Bath yesterday evening and was expected to be away at least three days. He was going with a party of other young gentlemen to visit Stonehenge or some such place.

So that was no good. Honor thanked the woman and went slowly back towards the theater. If only she could get hold of some member of the company . . . It was a pretty forlorn hope at that hour in the morning, and in fact the only person on view was an old woman scrubbing the steps. She did not know where any of the actors lived but thought that most of them came over on the coach from Bristol.

Honor walked on automatically and came to a halt on the corner of Queen Square because she did not know what to do next. It was all very well to say she would go after the runaways, but what was the use of that if she did not know which route they had taken. There was no obvious road from Bath to Scotland, so the travelers would have several choices, especially if they did not much care where they crossed the border. She could never catch them unless she had some clue to go on. If she knew where Harris had hired his carriage, for instance, she could inquire where he was proposing to change horses the first time, and then follow him stage by stage. Unluckily there were so many posting houses and livery stables in Bath, and she had no idea which one he was likely to use. This was where Dick Lyman could have helped her, for there were undoubtedly some that kept better horses than others, and some that liked to send their teams on a particular road. A young man like Dick would know such things, he would have been able to go straight to the most likely places, instead of wasting valuable time. And he could have asked his questions casually, without rousing suspicion, whereas if she went round the stables of Bath, asking about a couple in a post chaise, people would soon smell out a scandal.

Everything is so much easier for a man, she thought resentfully. And then recalled some of the things Marcus had said last night...

Had she been rash and stupid? The answer was

plainly yes, or that child of fifteen could never have made such a fool of her. She ought never to have trusted Henrietta, she ought to have guarded her a great deal more efficiently. Wise after the event, she saw now that she ought to have tackled Harris and warned him off. She had not done so, because she had thought this would look like making too much of a harmless episode that would be better forgotten. Above all, she ought to have written to Mrs. Porcheston about the Sydney Gardens adventure and so safeguarded her own position and Lucy's. She knew why she had kept quiet: Mrs. Porcheston would probably have removed Henrietta from the dangers of Bath, and they couldn't afford to lose her.

So now they would lose everything, the school would be ruined by the scandal, and as for that miserable girl, her future did not bear thinking of, married to such a scoundrel. If he did marry her, for it suddenly struck Honor that he might very well be married already. In which case they wouldn't be on the way to Scotland, they might be anywhere.

Oh God, what am I to do? thought Honor in despair. How am I to trace her?

PART SIX

Fox and Geese

The elopement had started badly. Henrietta, believing she was going to Scotland in a post chaise, decided to take as many of her clothes as she could. Stealing out of the house in the early morning, she staggered to the bottom of Guinea Lane carrying her dressing case, a bandbox, and an untidy bundle wrapped up in a shawl.

When Dick drove up in his curricle, there was a good deal of explaining to be done.

"Where's the carriage? I thought you said—"

"There isn't a carriage. I've had some bad luck. There was a low sort of woman at my lodging who turned out to be a thief, and she stole all the money I'd saved for the journey."

"Poor Dick, how dreadful! What are we to do? We can't go all the way to Scotland in that thing."

"We aren't going to Scotland. Now don't make a scene about it, there's a good girl. We're going instead to that house of your grandfather's in Gloucestershire, just for a short time, until I can raise some more money. I suppose you know how to get there," he added as an afterthought.

"I'm afraid I don't. The house is called Greengrace Manor, but I've no idea what part of the county it is in."

"Well, that's not much help. Still, it's an odd sort of name, and someone is bound to know. We shall have to make inquiries. Jump in, Hen, and don't dawdle." He then noticed the load she was carrying. "We can't take all that stuff in the curricle."

"I didn't know we should be in the curricle. You said you would have a chaise—"

"I didn't choose to be robbed," he said sulkily.

"I know, Dick. Don't be cross. Only I don't see what I am to do."

"Leave some of it on the pavement."

"I can't."

"Why not?"

"You can't just leave a bandbox on the pavement."

Dick jumped down from his high seat, thrust her belongings into every corner of the curricle, pushed her up after them, and climbed up again to join her. There was a sharp wind blowing along the street, the horses were fidgeting, and they had collected quite an audience of market porters and day servants going early to work. Dick was by now in a mood of extreme irritation.

"I am sorry to have brought so many dresses," she said coaxingly, slipping a hand inside his arm as they drove off. Dick did not respond.

She began to ask sympathetically about the theft of his money, and then wanted to know how he was going to get hold of a fresh supply. These were not questions Dick could very well answer. He could not tell Henrietta about the treacherous Clarinda, nor could he admit that the elopement plan had been financed from the start by his godmother Cecilia Porcheston, who had been paid to protect her from such perils. He did not feel like

159

inventing fairy stories. He had already had to compose one for his landlady when he left her house the day before, because he had been sharp enough to realize that Miss Clare might come running to consult him as Henrietta's cousin. Being without a bed to go to, he had sat up all night drinking and playing cards, so he was now very tired and not in the mood for sparkling conversation.

He told Henrietta not to chatter, and they drove in silence for several miles.

Presently she said, in a small, uncertain voice, "I hope you have not begun to regret the step we are taking."

"My dear girl—of course not! What a ridiculous idea."

He drew up by the roadside, took her in his arms and kissed her with a good deal of enthusiasm. After that things went better, and when they stopped to change horses at Nailsworth, Dick ordered breakfast in a private room and she was happy and excited to preside at what she thought of as the first meal of their life together.

Dick asked the way to Greengrace and soon afterwards their troubles began, for though they were given plenty of directions, these were all somewhat vague and mostly contradicted each other. Greengrace, it seemed, was a tiny village remote from any pike road. They found themselves driving interminably through a maze of little lanes, deep in long grass under leafy hedges, in a world where everything had gone to sleep. The view from the high seat of the curricle was very pretty, as Henrietta pointed out, but this did not pacify Dick, who grumbled continuously.

He grumbled about the hot weather, the dust, the

flies, the badness of the roads and the new pair of horses, slugs both of them. He was maddened by the ignorance of the few cottagers they met, and by Henrietta's dressing case, which kept shifting every time they turned a corner. He seemed to blame her for not knowing the way to a house she had never seen, even for having a grandfather who owned a house in such a stupid place.

Henrietta had never seen him like this before. She had never really seen him at all, having been completely dazzled by the surface of his personality: his extraordinary good looks and his engaging charm. Dick could be irresistibly charming so long as he was enjoying himself, as he had been able to do in Sussex and in Bath. Now life had become tedious and complicated. Here he was, landed with this helpless, unpractical girl, trundling around in search of a house that might not even exist, and conscious that if they had to go to an inn, his money would not last long.

"I can't think why you didn't have the sense to find out the way to this damned house of yours," he told her. "It was you who wanted to go there."

"Yes, and you said it would be a waste of time," retorted Henrietta, whose temper was being affected by his example. "Do mind how you drive. You nearly had us in the ditch."

This naturally annoyed Dick, who took the next bend much too fast, terrifying an old woman who was creeping along with a basket on her arm. She gave a scream and jumped into the hedge. The basket went flying.

"Silly old crone," muttered Dick, whipping up his horses to go on.

"No, no—you must stop, Dick. She may be hurt."

Dick had no intention of stopping, but Henrietta got hold of the reins and tugged at them, so that the horses shambled to a halt.

"You little idiot, you might have had us over!" he shouted.

Henrietta jumped down into the road and ran back to the old woman who was picking herself out of the hedge with groans and lamentations.

"I am so sorry. I do hope you are not badly hurt?"

"Lord-a-mercy, miss! I was never so frightened in all my days. My eggs all broke, that I was taking to my daughter—What am I to do?"

"I am so very sorry," said Henrietta again, looking at the chips of eggshell and the yolks congealing in the dust. "We must recompense you for your loss."

She went back to the curricle.

"I'm not giving her a penny," said Dick loudly. "It was her own fault. She must have heard us coming, she should have got out of the way."

Henrietta paid no attention. She reached for her reticule, and took out of her purse what she felt was the right amount to compensate the old woman, who seemed surprised and delighted.

"Bless you, my dear, for a sweet, pretty young maid."

As they drove off, Dick said crossly, "What's the point of throwing away charity on scum like that? Whiners and wasters the lot of them."

"I'm sure that's not true. My grandfather says most English people are very industrious, and anyway we should always take care of the poor because they have such hard lives."

"Your grandfather doesn't live in England," said Dick, scoring a point.

Henrietta said nothing. A new idea had come

162

into her mind. They had known all along that they would have to live on her money—Dick had not deceived her about that—and that it would come under his control once they were married. This did not worry her, and if he spent a certain amount of their income on hunting or racing without needing to ask her permission, she certainly would not grudge him these masculine pursuits. But it now struck her that when she eventually inherited her grandfather's estates, it would be very uncomfortable if she and Dick disagreed over the way the tenants were to be treated. The thought that their ideas might differ came as a distinct shock. She was still brooding over it when they came to yet another secluded village, with a church, and adjoining it, a moderate-sized stone house with mullioned windows and a steep gable.

"What's the name of this place?" Dick called out to a man who was scything the grass in the churchyard.

"Greengrace, sir," said the man, and seeing Dick was about to drive into the forecourt, he added, "There bain't no one lives there, sir, save Mrs. Drake. Manor's stood empty these ten year."

"Well, we are going there, nonetheless. The house belongs to General Delahaye, does it not? My wife's grandfather."

Dick shot a warning glance at Henrietta, as he made this premature announcement. They had not discussed how they were to describe themselves when they arrived at Greengrace, but she realized that it would have looked very odd and awkward to say anything else.

The man in the churchyard laid down his scythe, glanced with interest at Henrietta, and went to fetch Mrs. Drake, who appeared to be the caretaker.

Henrietta and Dick gazed about them. The color of the house was a pure, stately gray, quite unlike the golden stone of Bath. There were traces of an old formal garden submerged by weeds; bees hummed in the honeysuckle and the "proop proop" of pigeons echoed round an old dovecote. Everything shimmered in the slumberous haze of a July afternoon.

An elderly woman came out of the house, rubbing her red hands on her apron.

On seeing Henrietta, she forgot her prepared greeting and exclaimed: "God bless us, miss—you be the image of Mr. Henry!"

"Am I?" said Henrietta, pleased. Mr. Henry was her dead father.

"We'd no word you was married, miss—ma'am, I should say. What would your name be now, if I may ask?"

"Mrs. Richard Lyman." Her embarrassment at having to lie could have passed for the shyness of a bride.

The caretaker might be too simple to be surprised at the young couple driving about the country without even a lady's maid or groom, but when she heard they were expecting to stay at Greengrace, she protested in horror.

"But ma'am, it's not fit! There's no servants here nor furniture..."

"You cannot have received our letter," said Dick pleasantly.

"Letter, sir?"

"We wrote to tell you to expect us. (Did we not, my dear?) However, as you have had no
164

chance to make any preparations, we must camp like gypsies. It will suit us very well."

Having done his best to make their arrival seem a little less extraordinary, Dick walked into the house, with Henrietta beside him. The hall was very cool, deliciously so at first, though after a moment it felt too chilly for comfort. There were doors leading off into a series of low dark rooms, which were all perfectly empty, and all made gloomy by the bushes and creepers that grew up round the small windows, and by the shade of a great yew tree in the churchyard. The little panes of glass were thickly veiled in cobwebs.

"I did not know it would be like this," whispered Henrietta.

The dreariness of the house seemed to set the seal of failure on her elopement.

"You'd do better to come upstairs to the gallery, ma'am," said Mrs. Drake.

She was right. The small, sunny gallery was charming, the light streamed in from the south, and even though the air was full of dust, it was impossible not to admire the warmly glowing walls and the graceful plaster ceiling. Here Mrs. Drake brought them a hastily assembled meal: thick bread and butter with a basin of brawn and a slab of strong local cheese. There was a jug of home brewed ale and a pot of black, stewed tea.

Although there were no tables or chairs, there was space for them to sit on the broad window seat with the plates and dishes between them.

They did not talk much while they ate. They were too hungry, and besides, Mrs. Drake kept running about with a broom and a duster and hurrying into one of the adjoining rooms, her arms full of flapping sheets and blankets. Through the open door they could see what was apparently the one piece of furniture in the front part of the house: an enormous tester bed with bulging posts the size of young oak trees. Henrietta looked hastily away.

When they had finished eating, and Mrs. Drake had removed the remnants of their meal, there was a short silence.

"I'm afraid it is not quite what you—what either of us expected," apologized Henrietta.

"Well, we're here now, so it can't be helped."

It struck them both at the same moment that under the circumstances they ought not to care about their surroundings. Dick reached out a hand to Henrietta and she slid gratefully into his arms. He took refuge in the wordless language of kissing and caressing; it was the only language he had ever learned to speak to her, though neither of them had realized this.

Henrietta had been bewitched by the sensual enjoyment that Dick had given her, it was like a drug; each time they parted she began craving for the next time. In a sea of pleasure, she had hardly been aware of her own identity. Until now, when for some reason her mind seemed to be watching from somewhere outside her body, like a separate person—an entirely separate person from Dick, a stranger, who was rougher than usual and trying to do things he had never done before.

She shifted and pushed him back a little.

"What's the matter, sweetheart?"

"It's not very comfortable," she said, making the hard window seat an excuse.

"No, it isn't. If that old dame has finished making the bed, we may as well put it to use right away."

Henrietta sat up straight, bumping her head on his chin.

"Have I shocked you?" he asked, amused. "Going to bed in the afternoon is quite a fashionable pastime—and we are on our honeymoon."

"No, we aren't. A honeymoon doesn't begin until you've been married. We must wait, Dick."

He was incredulous and then outraged.

"Good God! What a little prude you are! Surely you don't intend to make me wait until we get to Scotland? We were as good as married directly we burned our boats and ran off together. Or don't you trust me to go through with the business?"

His eyes and mouth had become ugly, and for an instant she was not so much afraid as repelled.

"Of course I t-trust you," she stammered. "I'm sorry to be so disobliging, only I'm sure it would be wrong to do what you ask. A sin."

"A sin!" he scoffed. "I never heard such canting nonsense. What difference will it make to God or anyone else when you and I stand up in front of a couple of Scotsmen and declare ourselves man and wife? We aren't going to be married in church, you know. So you may as well give in straight away, you won't be any holier on the other side of the border."

She was confused and miserable.

"Please don't be angry with me, Dick. Give me time to think."

Dick stood up.

"Very well," he said, in a tone of deep displeasure. "You shall have the rest of the afternoon to come to your senses."

He stalked across the gallery and down the stairs.

2

About the time the runaways were breakfasting at Nailsworth, Honor was standing in Queen Square, desperately wondering how to set about finding them. If only she had not quarreled with Marcus Colvin! He would have known, better even than young Lyman, how to trace a carriage that had been hired in Bath this morning. Well, it was no use wishing, she could not crawl to him now, and after last night he would probably refuse to see her. Or would he? If she apologized and admitted that she had been unreasonable, it would be a tacit acknowledgment that some of the things he had said were justified. She had a fierce struggle with her pride, assuring herself that she could manage very well on her own. But she knew that Colvin's superior knowledge of the different stables and posting houses might produce much quicker results, and every minute saved could make a difference when it came to following a carriage on crowded roads, hoping it would be remembered by busy people like turnpike keepers and ostlers.

Mentally gritting her teeth, she walked briskly to the Crescent.

Marcus had taken the ground floor apartment of a house near the Brock Street end. Honor was shown into a large room where he was walking about with a coffee cup in his hand, surveying a table covered with books and papers. He was wearing some kind of oriental dressing gown made of silk and brilliantly striped in green and gold, which reminded her of the suspicious, foreign-looking man in the violet coat—though such exotic plumage was quite permissible in a dressing gown.

He was extremely surprised to see her, and showed it.

"You may wonder at my calling, Mr. Colvin," she began stiffly, "and I had much sooner not have come."

She paused, aware that this was hardly conciliating.

He said quickly, "Something has happened—an accident? Is it Sally?"

She now found herself apologizing for something quite different.

"It is nothing of that kind; Sally is perfectly well, I assure you. I am sorry to have given you such a scare. I should have realized how it must seem, my coming here at such an hour. But we are in great trouble and I need your advice. Henrietta Delahaye has eloped with Samuel Harris, the actor."

"Good God, what a stupid thing to have done. Surprising, too. Of course I will help you in any way I can. Do sit down and tell me all about it."

She told him the whole story, ending, "I don't know where to start my inquiries, and that is where I need your help. I tried to get hold of Henrietta's cousin, but he's gone off with a party of friends to Wiltshire."

"Oh? I suppose that's why he tried to borrow some money from me yesterday."

Honor was not much interested in Dick Lyman. She was embarrassed by having to acknowledge how badly she needed a man to help her, and could not avoid noticing how generously Marcus behaved over this. There was no mean triumph, not even a trace of satisfaction.

"I'll try the White Hart first, then the York or

the Christopher. If you go home, I will come and see you as soon as I have anything to report."

"Thank you," she said. "And thank you also, for being so magnanimous. I'm afraid I was dreadfully disagreeable last night."

"Yes, but you had a great deal of provocation," he said, smiling. "I'm glad to have the chance to make amends."

When Honor got back to the school, she heard a chorus of young voices declaiming the capital cities and rivers of Europe. Lucy was making a gallant effort to keep up the daily routine as though nothing was wrong. Outside the schoolroom door Nancy was standing with her back to the wall—sent out of the room for some petty crime.

"What have you been doing, Nancy?" Honor asked automatically. She was too preoccupied to be really interested.

"Miss Fielder sent me out for talking in class. Can I ask you something, Miss Clare? Is it true that Henrietta is supposed to have run away with Sam Harris?"

"That is no concern of yours," said Honor austerely.

"I don't believe it anyway. She doesn't care two straws for him. She is in love with Dick Lyman."

Honor was on the point of going into the parlor and closing the door behind her. She felt her spine prickle.

Turning, she said to Nancy, "Come in here and tell me why you think she doesn't care for Mr. Harris. She has not confided in you?"

"She told me she thought his acting rather ridiculous, if you call that confiding. She has always laughed at him. Only Martha is quite stupid about

170

him, and we could not resist teasing her a little. Not unkindly, you know, she didn't mind. That was what Hen was doing when she fell in the river. And then when poor Mr. Harris fished her out and got his beautiful clothes all muddied, Hen and I could not look at each other, we were laughing so much."

This account rang so true, so much truer, somehow, than the vision of Henrietta succumbing to her brave rescuer, that Honor almost laughed, herself. It was very reprehensible, a girl of Nancy's age had no business to be talking of such things. But Nancy was very acute, much cleverer than Martha, and, possibly, than Henrietta herself.

"Have you any real reason to suppose she is in love with her cousin?"

"Dick isn't her cousin, Miss Clare."

"Nonsense, of course he is! Her guardian told me so."

"No, truly. Hen said there was a mistake, though she could not understand how it came about. Dick is the godson of that lady she was living with in Sussex. You can ask Martha, she'll bear me out. Hen was already sweet on Dick when she came here—and it was Dick she went to Sydney Gardens with the other night, because I saw them walking down Belmont together from my bedroom window."

Honor was bewildered. Could this extraordinary story be true? It too was convincing, and accorded better with her own observations than the legendary passion for Harris. And what was this tax about them not being cousins?

She looked doubtfully at Nancy, remembering her past record.

"Will you promise me that you are telling the

truth? This is too serious a matter for playing tricks."

"I know how serious it is, otherwise I shouldn't be telling tales. My mother was like Hen, she was very pretty and she used to slip out secretly to meet my father. She was *imprudent,*" Nancy spoke the ambiguous word with a savage derision unnerving in anyone so young. "And when my grandfather found out, he made them get married to save her reputation. Only it was too late, I was born in six months, so there was quite a scandal after all, and she wouldn't have me in the room or look at me. She's hated me ever since."

Honor was thunderstruck. "My dear Nancy, I'm sure that cannot be true; that your mother hates you, I mean..."

She caught the expression in Nancy's eyes, the contempt of an honest person who was being lied to, and the conventional reassurance died away.

So this explained the unloved and unloving young creature, hostile yet forlorn, who had arrived here in the spring. How could her parents be so cruel? And irrational too, for in spite of their forced marriage, they seemed to be living together quite happily, with several younger children they were fond of.

"Will you go after Hen and bring her back?" asked Nancy, returning calmly to the main object.

Honor dragged her wits together. "Yes, if I can discover which road they have taken. Do you think Martha is likely to know anything?"

When she was consulted, Martha confirmed what Nancy had said, but knew nothing more. Lucy was horrified by Henrietta's duplicity, though after rereading the farewell letter she pointed out something they had not noticed before.

172

"She doesn't actually say whom she is going to marry. She says she is sorry to have deceived us about Sam Harris (which she certainly did, pretending she went to the Gala with him) and that she is going to Scotland to be married. What a little hypocrite!"

Honor and Lucy spent some time writing to Mrs. Porcheston; it took all the diplomacy they could muster.

They had barely finished when Marcus walked in, no longer dressed as a Sultan but as an English country gentleman in breeches and top boots.

"How glad I am to see you!" exclaimed Honor, jumping up.

"No news so far, I'm afraid, but it has just struck me that most of the actors live in Bristol, so Harris might have hired a carriage from there."

"Harris doesn't matter any more—that's what I wanted to tell you. She hasn't gone off with Harris, she's gone with Dick Lyman."

"How very odd. Did she change her mind?"

"No, of course not. She set out to make fools of us and we fell into the trap."

He interrupted only once while she was explaining, and that was to say, on a sharp note of inquiry, "Mrs. Porcheston's godson?"

"Mrs. Porcheston is the lady in whose family Henrietta was living in Sussex. She brought her here and made all the arrangements."

"Now I begin to see..."

He sounded so grim that she turned to him curiously, wondering what he meant by that enigmatic remark.

"That young scoundrel tried to borrow some money off me," he said. "I'm glad to say I turned him down. He told me he'd been robbed, but I thought there was something in his manner—that he was up to no good, and of course I was right. He wanted the money to elope with Henrietta."

"What impudence, expecting you to stake him!"

"Yes, wasn't it? However, I now have something useful to tell you after all. While I was at the White Hart I heard by chance that Lyman had ordered a post chaise for this morning, canceled it, and taken his curricle instead. He asked for details of posting inns on the Gloucester road. What do you make of that?"

"Surely he cannot mean to take her all the way to Scotland in that flimsy little open carriage," said Lucy.

"Not if he's short of funds. They'll want somewhere they can live very cheaply. Or better still, free."

There was a thoughtful silence.

Then Marcus said, "General Delahaye has a house in Gloucestershire."

"How do you know?" asked Lucy.

He did not answer directly, and Honor, more worldly than Lucy, thought that this was the sort of thing men of a certain position in society did know about each other, even without being personally acquainted.

Marcus said, "The name of the house is Greengrace Manor, and if Henrietta is there, we will go and fetch her back. We'll drive out along the Gloucester road and I am sure we shall soon get news of them."

"That's very kind of you," said Honor, torn between gratitude and diffidence. "I hardly like to accept. Because one of our pupils has gone astray, that is no reason why you should be expected to play fox and geese half across Gloucestershire."

174

"I shall be delighted to rescue your silly little goose from that particular fox. I feel partly responsible for her plight."

"But that is nonsense. How can you feel responsible?"

There was a brief pause.

"You can put it down to my passion for interfering," said Marcus Colvin.

(3)

Half-an-hour later Marcus was back to fetch Honor in a hired carriage. It was the barouche he had driven on the day of the picnic, and he had chosen it, he told her, in preference to a post chaise, because they did not want two gaping postilions to witness any awkward scene that might take place when they caught the runaways. She thought this very sensible.

They did not talk much at first. Honor was too wretched. She had managed to keep fairly hopeful while there were things to be done, plans to be made. Having to sit idle (even on the box of a fast-moving barouche) was the worst torment for a young woman of her temperament. As well as being anxious about Henrietta she had no doubt that a scandal over an eloping pupil would ruin her school. And if it was selfish to think about her own survival at such a time, she was bound to think about poor Lucy and about the other girls. Nancy, for instance. That pathetic revelation this morning had explained and even excused so much of Nancy's tiresome behavior. She had improved out of all knowledge in the last few weeks, and, if they could keep her long enough, Honor felt that she and Lucy could give her the judgment and

175

stability to face life philosophically, in spite of the wicked cold-hearted hypocrisy of her parents. This would require patience and growth. If Nancy was taken from them now, she would probably revert to her old unhappy self, and the same might be said of Evelina, so much better since she came to Bath. And as for the Marlows—what was to be done with them if the school had to close?

"Don't look so sad," said Marcus. "I'm sure we'll get her back."

"I do trust we shall. I'm very fond of Henrietta (though I could murder her at this moment) and clearly we are to blame for not looking after her properly."

"The odds were against you, I see that now."

"I wish I did. Not that it makes any difference, I must stop blaming other people for my own shortcomings. I lay awake last night, thinking over what you said—"

"So did I, and I came to the conclusion that all those names I called you: quixotic, obstinate—"

"Pig headed."

"Did I say that? How inelegant, I beg your pardon. And yet, you know, they are all qualities I particularly admire."

She could not help laughing, and glanced sideways at him, outlined against the sky. They were bowling smoothly along an open stretch of road, the horses were moving well and the hand holding the reins lay easily against his knee. He had regained his power over her without apparently making the slightest effort. Better not think of that now, this was no occasion for dalliance, and indeed the liveliness had died out of his expression. He looked remote, even grim.

After a moment she said, "I was racking my

brains to know what I am to do about the Marlow girls if the school should fail."

"Fail! We're not going to let it fail," he retorted, looking for some reason grimmer than ever. "Come, it is not like you to be so faint-hearted. Where's your Irish fighting spirit?"

She bit her lip but did not answer.

"I'm sorry," he said in a different voice, "I didn't mean to taunt you. Tell me what is so particular about the Marlows; I know their parents are in India, but they must have relatives in this country?"

"That's just it. I don't know."

She found herself telling him about the Marlows, how delightedly she had accepted them when the school was so short of pupils, without realizing that the money Mr. Marlow pressed into her hand would cover their fees for only one term. And how he and his wife had left no address she could apply to, not even their destination in India.

"It's the devil of a problem, isn't it?" he said. "What do you mean to do with them in the summer vacation?"

"Keep them with us in Belmont. I don't grudge them that, but I can't think what is to become of them eventually, even if we manage to avoid a scandal over Henrietta."

They had reached a toll gate, and as Marcus reined in and paid to go through, he asked for news of the runaways, whom he described as his young nephew and niece. Yes, they had been seen. Their combined good looks and Henrietta's red hair made them an easily-remembered pair. From then on, Marcus stopped at every respectable inn they passed, in the hope of learning something useful. At Nailsworth he got what he wanted.

"They breakfasted here," he announced, rejoining Honor, for whom he had ordered a glass of lemonade. "And Lyman asked the way to Greengrace. So now we know for certain where they are going. The village is some way off, but you will have Henrietta safely under your wing in a couple of hours."

Presently they left the pike road. It was by now very hot and the bumpy lanes, with their constant bends and turns, grew tedious. Honor and Marcus were too stoic to complain, neither wishing to add to the other's discomfort, though Honor found it difficult not to keep asking when they would arrive. It was a relief to know that she would be with Henrietta before nightfall, but the lovers had been alone together since six o'clock this morning; Honor could not help recalling the *imprudence* of Nancy's mother as she wondered what Henrietta was doing at this moment.

Henrietta was still in the gallery, staring down, disconsolate, into the neglected garden. She did not really see the uncut hedges, the urn overturned in the grass, the broken sundial lost under a cascade of white roses. She was still thinking over what Dick had said, and beginning to think that perhaps he was right. Their running away together had made their marriage inevitable, no other honorable course was open to them. So were they just as much married now as they would be after the formal declaration on Scottish soil? She was inclined to think so, and this should have eased her conscience and made her quite happy. Instead she now felt more miserable than before, faced with the dreadful suspicion that she did not really want to marry Dick after all. What had happened to her? Surely she wasn't so fickle and frivolous that she had stopped loving him because he had been cross and unkind? Anyway it was too late to change her mind, she had left Bath with Dick, and she would have to marry him or be disgraced forever. She did toy with an idea of creeping out of the house and losing herself in the woods and fields, but with hardly any money and nowhere to go, she might soon be worse off than she was now. Besides, it would be a cowardly thing to do, unworthy of a Delahaye.

If only Dick came back in a better temper, everything might still be all right. She went into the room where the bed was, and where all their baggage had been put; Mrs. Drake had brought in a basin with a jug of cold water. Henrietta decided to wash her face and hands. Having done so, she found there was no towel; her skin would have to dry in the warm air. She hunted for a comb and a looking glass, and went over to the window where the light was better. It was so odd being in a house with no furniture, but she could use the broad windowsill as a dressing table, pushing aside Dick's driving gloves and pistols that were lying there already.

Dick was sitting in an alehouse called the Green Man, at the far end of the village, writing a letter to his godmother.

When he had walked out of the gallery in high dudgeon, it had struck him that he ought to take this opportunity to find out about the coming and going of the mail, while Henrietta was not with him. He had not been able to write to Cecilia Porcheston from Bath, not knowing what address he should give for her reply. He could not risk receiving a letter at Greengrace Manor with the Brauncing postmark; Henrietta must never know that his godmother had planned their elopement from the start. It was so obviously a ploy to catch an heiress, even Henrietta would see that.

Parting with a coin from his shrinking store, Dick made sure that the local carrier would take his letter to the post town, and that he could use the Green Man as an accommodation address. He decided to write his appeal straight away—from what he had seen of the manor house he doubted whether there were any writing materials to be had.

The landlord supplied him with pen, ink and paper, and showed him into a stuffy room that smelled of ale and tobacco. And what would his honor like to drink?

"I've a good, strong ale, sir. I don't keep foreign wines, there not being any demand, but I've a few bottles of brandy that I got from an absentminded sailor who forgot to pay duty on them," said the landlord with a grin.

Dick asked for the smuggled brandy. It was crude, raw stuff but he needed it. As he wrote he drank, and as he drank he realized more and more how much he disliked women.

There was his godmother, petting and indulging him but always trying to manage him for his own good; wanting him to have a career, to improve himself, to make a great marriage. She had got him into this pickle and he couldn't even write and tell her how he'd lost the money she had given him. He'd have to invent a lot of silly lies or she'd start moralizing and dragging in his Poor Mama. Surely a fellow could amuse himself with a bird of paradise now and again, without being reminded of his mother's deathbed?

Only he hadn't amused himself with that damned

Clarinda. She had drugged him and robbed him without even performing the function she was paid for. Damn her and all the Jezebels like her who thought they could cheat him. And that included Henrietta.

By the time he had concocted a plausible letter and handed it over to be posted, Dick had begun to blame Henrietta for all the failings of Cecilia and Clarinda as well as her own.

He made his way back to the house, determined to show her who was master. Assert the rights of a husband, that was what he had to do, here and now, never mind all that legal mumbo jumbo about going to Scotland. And if Henrietta tried to refuse, so much the worse for her.

Breathing hard, he lunged his way clumsily up the stairs.

Henrietta was still standing by the bedroom window, nerving herself for their next encounter. Dick pushed open the door.

"Got over you pious fit, I hope?" He managed to focus her within his bloodshot vision. "I'm goin' teach you to be a good wife. We'll have an undress rehearsal."

"No, we won't," said Henrietta, taking in his condition. She was frightened but no longer undecided. She had no intention of going to bed with Dick while he was drunk.

Backing against the windowsill, her hand touched something cold and metallic.

"I warn you, Dick—if you try to ravish me, I—I'll shoot you."

The barouche, grey with dust, came into the courtyard.

"This must be the place," said Marcus...

From an upper window there came the unmistakable sound of a shot.

Marcus flung the reins into Honor's lap and jumped down from the box before the wheels had stopped turning. Telling her to look after the horses, he ran into the house.

(4)

The horses did not need looking after; they were tired and quite content to graze on a patch of rank grass round the front steps. Honor looped the reins over an iron lamp standard and followed Marcus. She ran up a dark staircase, across the bright stripes of sunlight in a deserted gallery and towards a room at the far end.

She could hear Henrietta's cry of anguish. "Oh God, I've killed him! I didn't know the gun was loaded."

Inside the room Dick Lyman was lying on the floor, chalk white and motionless, with his eyes closed, and a trickle of crimson spreading down his chest. Henrietta was kneeling on one side of him, she still held the smoking pistol. On the other side, Marcus was also kneeling, with his hand pressed against the wound, which seemed to be up near the shoulder.

He said, "I need a bandage. Quickly."

Honor saw the bed, turned back the covers, and began to tear at one of the linen sheets. It was very old and frail, the threads split easily between her fingers.

"I didn't mean to kill him," repeated Henrietta on a high, hysterical note.

"He's not dead," said Marcus.

As if to prove it, Dick began to groan, and tried to raise his head, retching ominously.

Henrietta implored him to say he forgave her, which was quite beyond him at present.

"Get the girl out of here, will you, Honor," said Marcus. "And pass me that basin before you go."

Honor did as she was told. Outside the door they met the elderly caretaker, who must also have heard the shot. Marcus sent her for hot water. He seemed perfectly competent to deal with the wounded man, which was a relief to Honor; her place was clearly with Henrietta, who clung to her like a lost child.

"Oh, Miss Clare, I am so glad to see you! It's like waking up from a nightmare—I thought Dick would bleed to death, and truly I never meant to hurt him. Only I wouldn't let him make love to me while he was drunk—and indeed he has been perfectly horrid to me all day. I'm sure he does not care for me in the least, and I don't think I can be in love with him either, for although I don't want him to die, I would much rather never see him again. I thought we were going to be so happy," wailed Henrietta, "but it was all quite different from what I expected."

Honor allowed her to talk on, thinking this would relieve her pent-up feelings. Badly as Henrietta had behaved, it was impossible not to pity her now, pinched and white, her beauty shattered by the shocks of the day. Honor was unable to crush the poor little culprit with a stern moral lecture, though she supposed it was her duty to do so. Instead, she sat holding Henrietta's hand and listening to an account of the elopement; it sounded to her as though Henrietta had probably been punished enough.

"How did you find me, Miss Clare?" Henrietta asked presently. "I did not think anyone in Bath knew about this house of my grandfather's. It was very clever of you."

"Yes, I think so too. Considering the trouble you took to convince us you had run away with Mr. Harris."

Henrietta flushed scarlet.

"I know how shockingly I have acted towards you and Miss Fielder," she said in a low mortified voice. "And when you have both been so kind to me. I am more ashamed of that than almost anything."

"But why did you try to mislead us? What was the point?"

"Dick wanted me to. He said it would give us a better chance of getting to the border without being caught—that was before he had his money stolen. I thought it was wrong and silly, only somehow I always did what Dick said. As though I was bewitched."

"The spell is broken now?"

Henrietta shivered. "Yes, quite broken."

The caretaker came back with a kettle; Marcus summoned her into the bedroom and presently there were sounds suggesting that Dick was being hoisted on to the bed. He groaned and cried out a great deal and Honor saw Henrietta wince at every groan.

"Shall we go outside?" she suggested. "The fresh air will do you good."

The great yew tree in the churchyard cast its pool of shade over one corner of the garden, where they found an old stone bench green with moss and lichen. Sitting there and contemplating the miniature jungle that had once been an herb garden, Honor forced herself to ask the essential question.

"There is one thing I must know, Henrietta. It is important that you should tell me the truth and at once; putting it off will only make things worse. Has Dick made love to you, either today or at any other time? You understand what I am talking about; not just kissing. Did he seduce you?"

"No, I promise you he didn't," said Henrietta earnestly, her eyes round and childish. "I wouldn't have agreed—though I must say, he never tried to. Not until this afternoon, and then he said that once we had eloped we were as good as married."

Honor believed her. The pistol shot seemed to provide confirmation. She was immensely relieved.

"Will there be a dreadful scandal?" asked Henrietta.

"I hope not. Mr. Colvin and I worked out a convincing story as we came along; you wanted to visit Greengrace, which has belonged to your family for so many centuries. I came with you as your chaperone, and we were escorted by Mr. Colvin and Mr. Lyman. Somehow we lost each other on the way, perhaps through taking a wrong road, but we are now reunited and we will return to Bath together. I don't know what we are to say about Dick's injury, though I am certain Mr. Colvin will think of something."

Marcus came out presently to join them.

"How is your patient?" asked Honor.

"He'll do. You will be pleased to hear that he said in front of me and Mrs. Drake that he was alone in the room when he carelessly dropped one of his pistols; he had forgotten it was loaded. As the good woman saw him come in three parts drunk, she was not unduly surprised."

"It was noble of Dick to exonerate me," said Henrietta gravely.

"Not really. I had already pointed out to him that he might easily be charged with abduction. It would not sound well for Master Dick that a fifteen-year-old girl found it necessary to shoot him."

Henrietta got up abruptly and moved away; she stood some distance off with her back to them.

"That was cruel," said Honor.

"Cruel to be kind. She's got over her infatuation for the young scoundrel; for heaven's sake don't let her start to imagine he's being *noble*. He's the most shocking coward, by the way. I tried to dig the bullet out of his shoulder and you never heard such an outcry. I had to give it up in the end. I gained a good deal of experience with gunshot wounds during my adventures in Greece, but this one is a little beyond me."

"Ought we not to send for a surgeon?" Honor asked in alarm.

"I don't want to do that because I have no idea whether the local man is any good. A clumsy butcher might start up the bleeding again, or go in too near the lung. What I'd like is to wait till the morning, and if he is fit to travel, take him back to Bath with us and get a first-rate man to attend him. We can't afford to have him dying on our hands."

"I should think not. Are you sure he will be safe until tomorrow?"

"Oh, I've got him well strapped and padded, he won't lose any more blood. But we shall have to spend the night here, I'm afraid. The horses must be rested. I hope you don't mind. You and Henrietta will be able to chaperone each other, nothing could be more respectable."

"Of course it will be respectable, now that I am here to take care of Henrietta. I don't need a duenna, myself."

"You are mistaken," he said coolly. "With young Lyman out of commission, Henrietta is a good deal less vulnerable than you are."

As Honor could not think of a suitable reply to this remark, she pretended not to have heard him.

The night they spent at Greengrace was not romantic. Rustic simplicity and ancient Gothic grandeur might be charming to read about in novels, but it was not at all comfortable camping in a house which had practically nothing in the way of tables or chairs, sheets or blankets, lamps, candles, china, glass or even knives and forks. Mrs. Drake, now thoroughly flustered, sent up a dish of tough mutton and watery potatoes. Her son Ben, who lived with her, was told to look after the horses. There were some truckle beds in the attic, once used by long-ago housemaids, and here Honor and Henrietta were invited to sleep, under the baking heat of the roof, after they had washed in a pail of tepid water carried up by Marcus from the kitchen. Henrietta did eventually get to sleep. Honor spent a good deal of the night on the floor below, taking turns with Marcus to watch by Dick's bedside, to make sure that he did not tear off his bandages and start the blood flowing once more, for he kept peevishly complaining that they were too tight.

Throughout all these difficulties Marcus was wonderfully patient and good-tempered. Besides looking after the invalid, he rubbed down and fed all the horses (for Ben Drake was not much better than an idiot) and when it was his turn to rest, he managed with a carriage rug on the gallery floor.

Even then Honor had to wake him to help her change Dick's bedding which was drenched with sweat. "I am so sorry," she said, leaning over him with a candle. "I didn't want to disturb you, but I don't think I can manage alone."

He sat up at once. "You were perfectly right to call me."

They had to turn the sheets round in the bed and use them again, for there were none to spare. Performing this menial task, Honor felt a curious closeness and affection between herself and Marcus, quite unlike the subtle excitement she had felt before. She thought this might be how married people felt during some of the frequent and testing episodes in their lives that had nothing to do with passion or pleasure.

They were afraid Dick might become feverish, but their careful nursing was rewarded; in the morning he was a good deal better, and Marcus considered him well enough to travel.

As the horses were now rested, they were able to make an early start. Marcus and Honor had decided that he should take Henrietta on the box beside him, while she traveled inside the barouche with Dick propped up as comfortably as possible.

Honor did not enjoy the journey. She wondered how she could ever have liked Dick Lyman. She was not simply disgusted by the whole episode of the elopement and his treatment of Henrietta; he was so vain and feeble, such a whiner. He tried hard to arouse her pity. A brave smile flickered across his pale face, as he said he had been foolish to expect strength of character or fidelity from a very young girl. . . . "They are the virtues one finds in an older woman."

"Are they?" inquired Honor, twenty-four to his twenty-one. "Older women can also be dangerous to young men like you."

"In what way, Miss Clare?" a challenge gleamed under the long eyelashes.

"Older women are much more likely to recognize heartless self-interest and sentimental cant."

She had no more trouble with Dick after that.

They reached Bath at about three, going first to Dick's lodging, where they handed him over to the care of his landlady, a motherly woman who doted on him, and who promised to send for the city's leading surgeon.

Marcus then drove Honor and Henrietta to Belmont. They were being watched for, and had hardly drawn up in the street when Lucy came running out of the house and down the steps from the high pavement.

"Henrietta is with you!—Oh, thank God! Her grandfather has arrived in Bath, he seems to know something of what has been going on and he is terribly angry!"

PART SEVEN

Aspects of Ruin

"How could Grandpapa know I had run away with Dick?" asked Henrietta fearfully.

They were all in the parlor now, including Marcus, who had whistled up a horsey-looking idler in the street to mind the barouche.

"He didn't know that when he got here," admitted Lucy, "though I'm afraid I was obliged to tell him; I had no choice. Only he seemed to be already convinced that you were being allowed too much liberty, not sufficiently protected—apparently someone has written to tell him the most dreadful stories about us, that we are not fit to keep a school, and he says he will see we never get another pupil!"

Lucy turned despairingly to Honor, who found herself once again facing the threat of total ruin. Having recovered Henrietta before she became either Dick's mistress or his wife, she had hoped that the danger was over. They had been bound to inform Mrs. Porcheston, and Henrietta herself would be taken away, but surely there would be no worse consequences. Suddenly everything was far more serious.

"Where is General Delahaye staying?" asked Marcus.

"At the White Hart. He said he would call here again at five, in case we had any more news."

Honor's mind was working hard. She said to Marcus, "I wonder if you could be here when the General comes? You would lend me so much support."

He was startled. "I hardly think . . ."

"Shall I have to see my grandfather?" faltered Henrietta, plainly terrified.

Kind-hearted Lucy said, "He is very anxious about you, and he will want to be sure you are safe. You will feel much more ready to meet him when you have had a rest. And something to eat, I dare say. Shall we go upstairs?"

"Yes, that is a very good idea," said Honor, who could see that this program would have a calming effect on both Henrietta and Lucy.

When they had gone, she said remorsefully to Marcus, "The child never even thanked you for all you have done for her."

"There was not the smallest need."

"Of course there was. If you hadn't driven me to Greengrace, that wretched young man might very well have bled to death, and where would she have been then? You saved his life, and I know she is not ungrateful—simply tired out and frightened of her grandfather, as I am myself. He sounds very fierce. Which is why I have had the temerity to ask one more kindness of you, in spite of all you have done for us already. General Delahaye seems to have got hold of some malicious rumor about the school—I don't know what it can be—but since we were careless enough to let his grandchild elope, it is going to be rather hard to prove that we are not always so incompetent. You are the father of one of our other pupils, the only parent within reach. Would you be prepared to tell the General that you are content to leave Sally in our care?"

He was strangely disconcerted by this appeal. "Of course I am content, though I doubt very much whether my saying so would have any effect—he would consider it an impertinence—in any case, what are you afraid of? He threatened to ruin you while Henrietta was missing; now she has come back safe and sound, and he can't make a scandal without involving her. The very last thing such a man would wish to do."

Honor said slowly, "He may not start the sort of scandal that would actually induce people to take their daughters away, but he can do something just as damaging. According to Lucy, he is making an unspecified attack; he is a distinguished man, he is staying at the most fashionable hotel in Bath. You know what a hive of gossip this place is. If word gets back to any of the tradesmen I owe money to, they will begin to dun me and I shall be finished."

"Are you in debt?"

"Yes. It's my own fault, I'm not going to blame anyone else or make excuses. I spent too much on decorating and furnishing this house, because I took it for granted that hordes of papas and mamas would be eagerly enrolling their daughters at my exclusive academy. I was conceited and silly. When we started with only seven girls, I wasn't able to pay all my bills. No one has pressed me so far; they calculate that if I succeed, I shall remain a valuable customer. But let the slightest hint get about that all is not well, and my creditors will want immediate payment."

She tried to speak lightly, too proud to let the

panic escape into her voice, and also feeling that he had heard quite enough of her troubles lately. Perhaps she acted too well; he seemed to take this disaster less seriously than the others.

"You are letting your fancy run riot," he said. "None of these terrible things is at all likely to happen, and I don't suppose you will find General Delahaye such a monster. Miss Fielder is inclined to be timid, being so gentle herself, but you will manage him very well, my dear Portia. May I call tomorrow and hear how you got on? I think I must leave you now, those horses ought to be fed and watered."

She had to let him go. She had no choice. Though she felt an acute pang of disappointment. Marcus had been such a tower of strength throughout their expedition to Greengrace, it seemed extraordinary that he should fail her now. Did he really not understand the fix she was in? Or did he not wish to be too closely associated with her, now they were back in the worldly and observant city of Bath? That idea hurt, even through all her other preoccupations.

She was wondering how to get through the next two hours, waiting for General Delahaye's visit, when it struck her that this was no way to conciliate the old gentleman. Somehow they had assumed that she had to receive him here at five o'clock, but of course he must be very anxious for news of Henrietta; it would be cruel to keep him waiting a moment longer than necessary. She would go at once to the White Hart and get the interview over—a plan which suited her much better than sitting here in suspense.

When she had changed her dress and told Lucy what she meant to do, she walked down to the hotel. It was in Stall Street, facing the Pump Room and the open collonade, with a view of the Abbey beyond.

She sent up her name, and was ushered almost immediately into a private parlor, where three people were sitting: a lady and two gentlemen. Seen against the light of the window, and through a haze of nervous apprehension, it was hard to make them out, but there was no mistaking General Delahaye, a small square man who jerked to his feet and advanced on her.

"Well, ma'am—where's my granddaughter?"

"Safely back in Belmont, I am thankful to say, sir. I found her in your house at Greengrace, only a few hours after she left us. She was perfectly well, though already regretting her foolish impulse."

"And you consider this a matter for congratulation? That she spent a whole day in the company of a lecherous young brute who had designs on her virtue—"

"I don't think you need worry, General. The young man had armed himself with a pistol for the journey; during the short time they were alone at Greengrace he let it off by accident and put a bullet in his shoulder."

She thought it best to give this version of the incident, at any rate in front of the General's two companions.

"Shot himself, did he?" growled Delahaye. "Saved me the trouble."

The lady by the window gave a cry of dismay. "He's not badly hurt?"

Honor was surprised to recognize Mrs. Porcheston. She said that Dick Lyman was in no particular danger, while wondering how Henrietta's

guardian could have reached Bath so soon from
Sussex—their express letter had been sent off only
yesterday. The third member of the party, a clergyman, was presumably Mr. Porcheston.

"I don't care whether the fellow's hurt or not,"
declared the General. "What I want to know is,
why the devil didn't you look after Henrietta properly, as you were paid to do?"

He glared at Honor. He had very blue eyes in
a face ravaged by time and tragedy; his white hair
might once have been as red as Henrietta's. Relief
had not softened his anger or his accusations.

"I've heard about you, ma'am, and your precious
school—place like a bear garden, young ladies
allowed to career about the public places of Bath
unsupervised, because you are too much the fine
lady to look after them. . . ."

Honor listened with a sinking heart. This was
worse than she had expected. What could he have
got hold of? An account of Nancy's wilder exploits
perhaps, exaggerated by some friend of his who
had been visiting Bath in the spring.

At last she felt impelled to make some sort of
defence.

"Whatever you may have heard, sir, I assure
you that Henrietta would not have been allowed
to meet Mr. Lyman if I had understood the danger.
I was told he was her cousin."

"Her cousin? She never told you that?"

"No, but . . ."

"Then he did, I'll be bound! Good God, ma'am,
are you fool enough to believe such a tale from
any scamp who presents himself at your door? And
you are supposed to be a protector of innocent
young girls. It seems to me that you have mistaken your profession."

Flushed with fury and humiliation, Honor retorted, "Naturally I am not as stupid as that. I believed he was her cousin because Mrs. Porcheston told me so."

She glanced at the woman on the sofa, who stared back at her with unblinking hostility and said, with cold self-possession, "I never told you anything of the kind."

For an instant Honor wondered whether she had made some terrible mistake.

"Then what was the name of the young man you said might be received as a visitor? Her real cousin?"

"There is no such young man, she has no cousin." Mrs. Porcheston turned to the General. "I cannot imagine what Miss Clare is talking about. I gave her particular instructions that Henrietta was to be most strictly chaperoned, not permitted to meet anyone outside the school—I hope you believe me, sir. It is bad enough to feel that I have made such an unfortunate choice of school, I admit I was completely taken in. Even so, I am astounded that Miss Clare should have the impudence to put the blame on me, just because Henrietta first met poor Dick in our house. And I'm sure they would never have behaved so badly if this wicked woman had not allowed them so much license. Which I certainly never did."

She dabbed her eyes with a tiny handkerchief.

"There, my dear. No one is blaming you," said her husband.

The General rounded on Honor.

"Do you seriously imagine that you are going to escape the consequences of your negligence? That you can preserve your character by telling lies?"

Honor realized she was in a trap. No one was going to believe her. Very dimly she began to perceive a little of what must have happened in the Sussex parsonage while Henrietta was in the care of Mrs. Porcheston, the doting godmother of Dick Lyman. And there was nothing whatever she could do to save herself from being made a scapegoat.

Standing there in a kind of stunned weariness, she heard the door open behind her, and saw, without much interest, that Mrs. Porcheston stiffened and gave a little gasp of surprise.

General Delahaye's manner changed too, he became suddenly genial.

"My dear fellow, I did not know you were still in Bath! I am very grateful to you, for everything you told me about that damned school is all too true. My poor little Henrietta has been a victim of the most disgraceful incompetence and folly!"

Honor was curious enough to look round and see who it was had blackened the reputation of her school.

The person who had come into the room was Marcus Colvin.

He saw her at the same moment, and was backing to the door with a horrified expression, as though he meant to bolt, when the General caught his hand and wrung it with enthusiasm.

"I am so sorry," said Marcus, apparently speaking to Honor. "I didn't think you'd be here—I'll explain later. My dear sir, I am afraid there has been a serious mistake. When I wrote to you about Miss Clare's school, I gave you a totally false impression. . . ."

Shock had made Honor feel unnaturally cold

and numb. Marcus had betrayed her. While pretending to be her friend, he had been abusing her to General Delahaye, whom he appeared to know quite well. Why had he never said so? And the Porchestons: apparently he knew them too. She watched and listened with the dulled comprehension of someone trying to follow a play in a foreign language, the full sense eluded her.

"I did not at first understand the situation," Marcus was saying. "The school so recently opened, the girls still strangers and one in particular most difficult to manage. Things are different now."

"That's all very well, Colvin. My granddaughter has been regularly meeting a young blackguard who was after her money."

"There was a special reason to account for that. Have you asked Mrs. Porcheston how she came to hear of Miss Clare and her school?"

They all looked at Mrs. Porcheston, who did not speak. She was unbuttoning her spencer as though she felt the heat.

"It was from Lady Midhurst, was it not, my dear?" prompted Mr. Porcheston. "She recommended the place when we called on her in London. I remember your telling me so, not at the time, but later; when we decided that Henrietta needed a change. You thought a spell in Bath might make her forget about Dick."

"Yes. Yes, I told you, didn't I? It was Lady Midhurst."

"I think you are forgetting, Mrs. Porcheston," said Marcus, "that I gave you a very unflattering account of the school the day I visited you at Brauncing."

"This is outrageous!" said Mr. Porcheston. "Are

you calling my wife a liar, sir? No such conversation ever took place."

"You did not hear it. We were walking back from the Abbey; I was beside your wife and you were some way ahead with Colonel and Mrs. Weldon."

"He's making it up," said Mrs. Porcheston rather faintly. "He's in league with that insinuating woman. He has no right to say such things, for he cannot have a vestige of proof."

"I am sorry to contradict you, ma'am," said Marcus, in a silky tone which suggested he was not in the least sorry. "I can give General Delahaye as much proof as he requires. I have just visited your godson Dick Lyman on his sickbed. He insisted that the idea of his eloping with Miss Delahaye came from you in the first place, and you chose the school because I had said that the girls were left to run wild. He says you sent him to Bath, having already informed Miss Clare that he was Miss Delahaye's cousin. You even promised to pay the expenses of the elopement."

The General rounded on Mrs. Porcheston, but her husband got in before him.

"Cecilia," he demanded in an implacable voice, "is this true?"

She was twisting the handkerchief round and round her fingers.

"Don't look at me like that, John. I never meant any harm. Why shouldn't poor Dick have his chance? The girl was mad for him, and he'd have made her a very good husband."

"And deserted her at the first sign of trouble, I suppose, just as he's deserted you. I am ashamed to think that you could be so wicked and so stupid."

"Oh! Oh!" cried Cecilia Porcheston, preparing to take refuge in hysterics.

General Delahaye approached Honor.

"I owe you a most humble apology, Miss Clare. I fear I have done you a grave injustice. My only excuse is that I have been misled—deceived by someone I thought I could trust."

Honor dragged herself out of her mute isolation.

"I understand perfectly, sir," she said quietly. "I too have been deceived by someone I thought I could trust."

(2)

"I do wish you would see him," said Lucy. "He has called here three times, besides writing that long letter you wouldn't read. He is so anxious to explain."

"I'm sure he is. He likes everybody to think highly of him, does Mr. Marcus Colvin. Well, he has won golden opinions from all sorts of people, including you and General Delahaye, so he can do without mine."

"You are very hard. If you would let me tell you how it was—"

"I don't want to hear how it was," said Honor, hard put to it not to scream. "I know enough already. He went round blackening our reputation to his influential friends; when he discovered that Henrietta had been placed with us, in spite of all his malice, he didn't think of warning me that something odd was going on. He sat back and let Dick Lyman run off with her, and then when he finally stirred himself to go after them, he allowed me to suppose that he was doing us a great service.

So he wants to explain, does he? Well, I dare say some of his actions can be logically explained, but nothing—*nothing* can excuse them!"

Lucy said no more.

It was two days since the revelations at the White Hart, and the house had been in a state of siege, with Marcus trying to see Honor, and Honor refusing to meet him. She had been deeply hurt, and she could not bring herself to think dispassionately, or to examine the motives for anything Marcus had said or done. He had made a complete fool of her. She had believed that he stayed on in Bath, and came so often to the house, because he was in love with her. Now it turned out that he had stayed to keep an eye on Henrietta, whom he believed to be in grave danger through Honor's incompetence. Sally too—he must have been watching over her. He would not like to leave her in such hands.

"Is he going to remove Sally?" she asked abruptly.

"He hasn't said so."

"He will. You'll see. He's making use of us until he can find something better."

Lucy looked with pity at her distracted friend and did not argue.

General Delahaye had called the day before, too full of his own apologies to be very severe with Henrietta, who cast herself into his arms in a suitably penitent state and promised that she would never, never elope with anyone again.

The General now showed a flattering desire to consult Honor and Lucy. He was thinking of reopening his London house and taking Henrietta to live there with him. What did Miss Clare and Miss Fielder think? There was an old friend of

201

Henrietta's mother, herself a widow with a daughter of sixteen; he hoped she would be willing to come and live in the house as Henrietta's companion-chaperone, taking care of both girls and presently launching them in society.

"I think it would be a very wise move," said Honor. "Henrietta has given us all a fright, sir, but I don't believe she is one of those silly, over-susceptible girls who are continuously getting into scrapes. I think what she wanted most from Dick Lyman was simply affection, only he was too stupid to realize that and play his cards properly. When she discovered how selfish and unkind he could be, she soon came to her senses."

"I ought to have made a home for her before," said the old man. "Instead of indulging my grief. I must do my best now. I believe Henrietta has made several friends here. A girl called Martha, and another—Nancy, is it? Something of a hoyden, I gather. Perhaps they can pay us a visit some time."

The idea of Nancy and the General in conjunction was rather awe inspiring. She would enjoy such an advantage, though, and so would Martha, if only they could fit her out with suitable clothes.

Another caller they felt obliged to receive was Mr. Porcheston. He and his wife were staying at the Belvedere Hotel, and he came down to Belmont to say, on her behalf, the things she would not or could not bring herself to say.

"I was horrified," declared the poor man, glancing from Honor to Lucy, "to discover that my wife could devise such a wicked plot against a child in our care, and then let it be carried out in a way that was likely to bring about the ruin of innocent people."

"I don't suppose she considered that side of it," said Honor. "It may not have struck her that the school would be so seriously affected."

"I'm afraid she would not have cared. She has never been quick to appreciate any trouble that does not affect us personally."

There was an uncomfortable pause. It was hard to know what to say to this pleasant straightforward man who was obviously so shaken by the knowledge that his wife had behaved like a criminal.

"However, she may soon be forced to contemplate poverty and hardship at close quarters," he said grimly. "As I have pointed out to her, if General Delahaye tells my patron, Lord Midhurst, what has happened, we may be turned out of the parsonage house at Brauncing and lose our income at one fell stroke."

"Oh, I hope not!" exclaimed Lucy. "It wasn't your fault."

"Not my fault! A clergyman who has been able to make so little impression on his own wife."

"But we are told that a prophet is without honor in his own country," Lucy blushed, adding, "I should not quote scripture to you, Mr. Porcheston."

"You have every right to do so, Miss Fielder, for you seem to be showing an admirable Christian spirit. And I don't think the General is going to tell Midhurst. So we shall probably go on at Brauncing—with one difference. I have told Cecilia that we will have nothing further to do with young Lyman. I don't want to be unduly hard, but I cannot have him forever about the place, venal and greedy, setting a bad example and perhaps corrupting my children."

It struck both Honor and Lucy that the person most likely to corrupt his children was their own mother.

"Poor man," said Honor, after he had gone, "I do pity him."

"I pity her too. It would be dreadful to lose the affection of such a man. I am sure she must feel it acutely."

"You would feel it, my dear Lucy, because you are so tenderhearted and so good. (And he is extremely handsome, isn't he?) I dare say Mrs. Porcheston is too self-centered to care, or even to notice what she has done to him."

Next day, however, Honor changed her mind. She was at the bottom of the Lansdown Road, waiting to cross, when a post chaise slowed down at the corner, preparing to turn left into the London Road as soon as there was a break in the traffic. Glancing casually into the window of the chaise, she saw one of the passengers leaning slightly forward and staring ahead. It was Cecilia Porcheston. She looked ten years older than the elegant creature who had interviewed Honor at the Belvedere Hotel, and later lied about their conversation. Her features were set with a look of endurance and bewilderment, as though she still did not understand why she was being made to suffer. Then the chaise jolted on, and the Porchestons were carried away from Bath and into the bleak privacy of their continuing marriage.

Honor was haunted by that cameo glimpse. When she had finished her errand in Milsom Street she went home, full of the Porchestons, to be met by Lucy who said that Mr. Colvin had called while she was out.

"I wish he would stop calling."

"He didn't ask for you," said Lucy, not without a faint trace of asperity. "He came to say goodbye to Sally. He is leaving for London immediately, and she is to travel up with the Delahayes when the holidays begin. The General has offered to take her."

General Delahaye was still at the White Hart and Henrietta spent a good deal of her time with him, though she continued to sleep at the school.

Honor peeled off her gloves and threw them down. Marcus Colvin cared nothing for her, and this proved it. If he had really wanted to see her again, he wouldn't have given in so easily and gone away.

The holidays would soon be here. The girls' clothes were being counted and checked, trunks brought down from the attic. The Roses and the Newlanders had made arrangements to fetch their daughters.

"If you please, Miss Clare, what is to happen to us?" asked Martha timidly.

"You are going to stay here with me and Miss Fielder. Don't look so downcast, my dear child—you will not have to do any lessons. We will make some expeditions into the country if the weather is fine: long walks and picnics."

Honor tried to sound more cheerful than she felt, though the mere thought of a picnic reminded her of a day she was trying to forget.

"It is very kind of you," said Martha in a tight breathless voice. "I am afraid Papa did not give you enough money to go on keeping us in the vacation, did he? I am sure we ought not to stay here, only we have nowhere else to go. You must tell me if we are eating too much."

"Don't talk such nonsense," said Honor quite sharply. "You can eat as much as you please. Your father and I fixed everything between us, and this is not a subject that girls of your age are expected to know about."

When Nancy heard of the proposed picnics, she said, "I wish I could stay at school, I don't want to go home, and I shall count the days to the beginning of next term."

"I'm sure you will be happier, Nancy, if you will just try to behave agreeably, as you have been doing here. Your parents will be pleased to see how much you have learned."

Honor had not yet managed to have a proper talk with Nancy about the difficulties in her family life and her vision of herself as an unwanted outcast. Nancy needed help, but Honor had not felt able to give it. Energy had drained out of her, and she had no initiative left for extra complications. When she heard Nancy talk about next term, she felt a pang of guilt, for she did not think there would be a school in Belmont next term for Nancy to come to.

Keeping the tradesmen at bay was not going to be enough, Honor had realized that now. Of the eight girls who had attended the school at its highest peak, Corisande had gone already, Henrietta and Sally would be going soon. That left five, including the Marlows, and the money their father had left was now at an end. No new inquiries had been received, and by next term the only paying pupils would be Nancy Newlander and Evelina Rose. Their fees could not possibly be stretched to provide for herself, Lucy, three more girls and the servants. What were they to do?

3

On the last afternoon of the term, Lucy took the girls to Sydney Gardens to explore the labyrinth, a long-promised treat. Honor did not go with them. She stayed at home to worry about her problems. She had not yet told Lucy how bad things were, though she had an idea that Lucy guessed, and that Martha, Nancy and even Margaret realized something was wrong.

Honor wandered about the house, restless and miserable. She went into the drawing room on the first floor which she had furnished with such loving care—and at such expense because it had been intended for parties and concerts where talented pupils were to be shown off to their proud and delighted parents. No entertainment had ever taken place. The kind of parents who patronize my school, she decided bitterly, don't expect to be proud of their daughters; they simply want them kept out of sight.

All my swans were geese, she thought, remembering the printed cards she had sent out so assiduously, and surveying the polished chairs and tables, the striped wallpaper, the china cabinet and the elaborately draped curtains. The chair seats and sofa had their covers on, but underneath was a delicious apricot silk, chosen to match the colors in the Axminster carpet, now nestling under its drugget. She thought of the pleasure she had felt, a few months ago, arranging this room, saw herself flashing about in a mood of bubbling overconfidence.

She did not know what was to become of herself, did not much care in her present state of mind, but she did care desperately about Lucy and about their five remaining girls, all so dependent and vulnerable.

There were sounds of an altercation in the hall, as though Pinker was trying to repel an unwelcome visitor. Following her recent train of thought, Honor had the horrid idea that she was being dunned by an impatient tradesman. She opened the drawing room door and listened.

A well-known voice was saying, "I know your mistress has given orders that she doesn't want to see me. She will, however, when she hears what I have to tell her."

Dodging round the faithful Pinker, Marcus took the stairs three at a time.

Honor met him at the top, cold with anger.

"How dare you force your way in here! Surely you must realize by now that I want nothing more to do with you."

"Don't you want to know the name of the man who is supposed to be acting as guardian to the Marlow sisters?"

She gazed at him in disbelief. "You don't mean to say you've found him?"

"I went to London solely for that purpose."

She walked into the drawing room and sat down. Marcus followed her, and as she did not offer him a chair, he remained standing, as she had been obliged to do on that terrible afternoon at the White Hart. This was not intentional, she had simply forgotten her manners.

"Who is he? How did you find him?"

"I called at the offices of the East India Company. I already knew from Martha the name of the ship her parents sailed on, so it was easy to make sure that Marlow has indeed been promised a minor post in Bengal, though exactly where he is to be sent will depend on circumstances when he gets there. This in itself is not much help to you, but while I was there an official told me that they had received letters from someone who was trying to locate Mr. Marlow's children. A Mr. Frobisher, a city merchant with premises in Leadenhall Street.

"I went to see Mr. Frobisher, and when he heard why I had come, I thought he was going to embrace me. He and Marlow are old friends. Marlow is, of course, a gamester, the sort of man who cannot keep a penny in his pocket but has an extraordinary gift for keeping his much-tried friends. They have frequently saved him from disaster, and at last, this spring, persuaded him that he must leave the country for his own good. They got him out of his latest difficulties, and obtained the post for him in India, Mr. Frobisher's contribution was to act as guardian to the little girls, give them a home during the holidays, and guarantee that their next school bills would be paid if no money had yet come through from India.

"A fortnight before Marlow and his wife were due to sail, there was another crisis. A new creditor turned up, with a very large outstanding debt which Marlow had forgotten to mention, and which none of his Good Samaritans felt able to shoulder. To make matters worse, this creditor was someone who does business with Frobisher, and who kept demanding from him where Marlow was to be found. Frobisher is one of those transparently honest men who hates telling lies, probably knows he tells them very badly. He sent a roundabout message to Marlow, imploring him to keep out of the way; he didn't want to know anything about any of the Marlows until after the

209

ship had sailed. All he wanted was the address of the children's school. He received an answer, but did not even open it until he had seen in the newspaper that the East Indiaman had sailed. It contained the address of a school kept by a Miss Barnstable in Queen Square, Bath."

"Miss Barnstable? I know her. But why did the Marlows—I'm sorry. Go on."

"Frobisher wrote to Miss Barnstable. She replied that the girls were not at her school. They had been expected, had actually arrived, but unfortunately she had not been able to meet Mr. Marlow's wishes in certain respects—I imagine he couldn't pay the full fees, though she was too discreet to say so. At any rate the parents and children had all gone away and she knew nothing more about them.

"Frobisher had been fretting himself into a shadow, wondering where the children could be."

"Did it never occur to him that they might be at another school in Bath?"

Marcus became deliberately vague. "He guessed, of course, that Marlow had run short of money as usual, and he said that if one school had refused to have the girls, it was not very likely..."

"That Marlow could have found anyone stupid enough to be taken in," concluded Honor. "But he did, you see. Wretched man—and he did not even remember to write and tell poor Mr. Frobisher the change of school. I know it all happened in a great rush, they told me there had been some disappointment at another school; I didn't grasp the implications at the time. Good heavens, do you think that poor woman may suddenly have realized, in the middle of the Indian Ocean, that they never gave Mr. Frobisher the new address?"

It was a disturbing thought, though anyone who had been married to Mr. Marlow for fifteen years must have developed a blind faith that there would always be someone else to clear up the train of havoc he left behind him. At least Martha and her sisters need no longer feel deserted and bereft.

"I am so thankful there is someone who cares about those girls. What is he like?"

"Frobisher? A very good sort of man. He has a wife and a house in Islington, and they have brought up daughters of their own. He is writing to you today, I believe."

"We shall be able to keep the school open after all!"

The fact had only just dawned on her.

Marcus frowned. "Are you in such deep water?"

"Yes. No. It's no business of yours—I do wish you would not tower over me in that inquisitorial way," said Honor crossly.

She could not bear him to know she was on the brink of failure.

"I haven't been invited to sit down."

"I beg your pardon, Mr. Colvin. Do take a chair."

He did take one, bringing it quite close to hers, and saying persuasively, "Won't you let me tell you about the Delahayes and the Porchestons—what really happened? I know I behaved shabbily and I shan't try to justify myself, but I cannot bear to see you looking so unhappy."

She wanted to send him away, but how could she, when he had just done her such a service? And besides, her voice might not be quite steady, and she didn't want him to misunderstand the reason.

So she said nothing, and he took the chance to begin.

211

"I came back to England in a frigate of the Mediterranean Fleet. We were caught in a violent storm, as I told you, and just managed to limp into port at St. Damien in the Scillies. That's the island where General Delahaye lives in a gloomy old fortress overlooking the harbor. He sent down to know if he could assist us. The captain went to pay his respects and took me with him. The result was that I visited the old man several times while the ship was repairing. After several years as a hermit, I think he was secretly longing to talk to someone from the outside world, and in spite of the difference in our ages, we found we had one thing in common: we were both widowers left with the problem of bringing up a young girl. Delahaye told me that his granddaughter was living with the Porchestons in Sussex.

"In due course we sailed for Plymouth, and you know what happened next: I heard from a family connection that Sally had been packed off to boarding school, and I descended on you here in a thoroughly bad temper. That was my fault, not yours. I was fighting off an attack of conscience. I knew I had neglected Sally after my wife died. I had left her with her aunt because it suited me, and when I discovered she had been sent away, I was furious. No matter what the school had been like, I should have found a hundred things wrong with it."

"We did make it easy for you," admitted Honor.

"Perhaps. But the final straw came when you refused—quite reasonably—to let me remove Sally without consulting Miss Butley. It showed me what an ineffective father I had been—as well as a bad husband—and that was intolerable.

"I had to make some other arrangement for

Sally, and I thought at once of the Porchestons, whom General Delahaye had praised so warmly. I had friends living near Brauncing, I invited myself to stay with them, and they took me over to the parsonage. We had not mentioned the real reason for our visit, which was just as well, for within thirty seconds of entering the house I had decided I was not going to place Sally in the care of Mrs. Porcheston. We overheard her scolding Henrietta in a voice of such cold unkindness that I knew for certain she would not do. We were obliged to get through the rest of the visit, walking round one of those dull medieval ruins that English people are so attached to," said Marcus, with the unconscious arrogance of a man who had been to Greece, "and on our way back I was beside Mrs. Porcheston when she said something about sending girls to school.

"I don't know what made me do it, but I began to give her a spiteful, exaggerated account of the school I had seen recently in Bath. I hardly knew her, and I didn't care for what I had seen, yet I could not resist the pleasure of talking in this way. I suppose it relieved my resentment, and she seemed to take a great interest in my conversation. Now I know why."

Marcus waited, perhaps expecting Honor to comment. She felt a kind of pain but ignored it; one could not call this a betrayal, at the time he had hardly known her. This was not what she held against him.

"I went back to London," he continued, "and tried to find some other school or family that would take Sally. I soon began to realize that I had been over-critical....I saw grim bastilles where the children looked sickly and defeated, fussy villas where they wasted their time cutting up silver paper and giggling. Nothing would do. I tried to engage a governess, but that was no good either. No young woman would accept a post where there was not a lady in the family, and the older ones objected because I had no proper establishment to offer, only the prospect of furnished lodgings. And they were such dragons!"

At this point Honor lost a little of her moral advantage by laughing.

"Yes, you may laugh. I came back to Bath in quite a different mood—and almost the first person I saw was Henrietta Delahaye. I had not met her at Brauncing, I simply saw her for an instant as she ran upstairs, too distressed to notice there was anyone in the hall. Still, she made a strong impression, and I was so taken aback that I actually asked her name, which was a false move, for you immediately started disapproving of me once more. You thought I was the kind of man who runs after pretty schoolgirls."

"I wasn't sure whether it was her looks or her money that attracted you."

Marcus said slowly, "You thought I was a fortune hunter?"

This, for some reason, seemed to have a curious effect on him. It was several seconds before he went on.

"You can appreciate now what a quandary I was in. I had given Mrs. Porcheston a highly prejudiced account of your school (without ever mentioning that my own daughter was one of the pupils or that I should shortly be returning to Bath).On hearing my description, she promptly sent Henrietta to you, as though she actually wanted the child to get into some sort of scrape. What possible motive could she have? And what ought I to do?

"General Delahaye had confided in me a little, I knew he was devoted to Henrietta. I felt obliged to give him a hint about the Porchestons, though it was decidedly awkward. He is not the sort of man who takes kindly to criticism or advice. And it was just possible I had misjudged Mrs. Porcheston: suppose she had received good reports of the school from some friend whose opinion was more valuable than mine? Coincidences do happen. In the end I wrote to the old man, said that I believed his grandchild was now at a certain school in Bath, and gave him a brief summary of my own opinion, formed a few weeks earlier. It was far more moderate than the exaggerated nonsense I had talked to Mrs. Porcheston, but I'm afraid it was—not complimentary." He shot her a doubtful, placating glance and hurried on. "I hoped this would put Delahaye on his guard, and that if he started asking questions, Mrs. Porcheston would be frightened out of any scheme she might be hatching."

"How soon did you write?"

"The day after I returned here. Before I had the chance to realize how unjust my first impressions had been."

"Then why did General Delahaye take so long to act?"

"Letters travel pretty slowly between the Scillies and the mainland, especially to the more remote islands. I gather he took some time considering the matter, writing to the Porchestons, feeling vaguely dissatisfied with their reply, before finally breaking out of his seclusion and coming over to England to see what was going on—and incidentally commanding the Porchestons to meet him in Bath.

"In the meanwhile Henrietta's so-called cousin had appeared, and here I was uncommonly dense. I did not see how his arrival could have any bearing on Mrs. Porcheston's strange behavior, because I accepted what you told me about him without ever considering that your information must have come from Mrs. Porcheston herself. Of course you trusted her, a lady of such immaculate respectability. I was the one who should have been more alert. When we thought that Henrietta had run away with Harris, I did not suspect Mrs. Porcheston's influence for one moment. It was when young Nancy came out with the truth, that the light finally broke on me. Most unpleasantly. That fiendish woman had made me an accessory unawares, and if poor little Henrietta was trapped into marrying Lyman, it would be largely my fault. I was lucky, however. I knew Lyman was short of money, and I knew the Delahayes had a house at Greengrace, I'd seen pictures of it in the library on St. Damien. We were able to recover Henrietta and I thought our troubles were over.

"Then we got back here to find that the General was in Bath, breathing fire and slaughter, and what the devil was I to do? You asked me to meet him with you, but how could I, without giving the game away? I felt a perfect brute when I refused, though I had begun to see a way out of my dilemma. He was to call on you here at five; that gave me about an hour to have a private inquisition with Lyman (which I had been promising myself anyway) and then go on to the White Hart and give the General the full explanation, pointing out how badly you had been treated, and that you were in no way to blame. Instead, you changed your mind and went to the White Hart ahead of me. So I was properly caught out, and I suppose it served me right."

While Marcus was speaking, Honor had been sitting very still with her hands in her lap, gazing across the room at a looking glass in a gilt frame on the opposite wall. It was hanging slightly crooked, and among all her feelings of discomfort and uncertainty, was an irritating desire to put it straight. Perhaps it reflected the world a little askew, like some aspects of his story.

He had come to the end, apparently, and was waiting for her verdict.

At last she said, "Do you still think that Lucy and I are negligent and incompetent, not fit to have charge of young girls? And that the place is no better than a bear garden?"

"Portia, you know I don't! I have the greatest admiration for the way you care for these children. You have worked wonders, especially with Nancy perhaps, but with the others too. It was only right at the beginning that I had that impression, and that was partly due to my own resentment—"

"Yes, I see that. And when you wrote to General Delahaye, you still didn't know us any better. But if you have really changed your mind during all these weeks we have been seeing so much of you, why didn't you write to him again and remove the bad impression you'd given him? You took us for the picnic, to Sydney Gardens, you seemed to—to like us so much, and all the time you let General Delahaye go on thinking that his granddaughter had fallen into the clutches of people who were quite unfit to take care of her."

"Well, so she had."

She caught her breath, ready to flare up again, confused and suspicious.

Marcus said, "Try to understand, my dear. I don't mean you and Lucy. I mean the Porchestons, or rather Mrs. P., for the parson was entirely innocent, poor man. She deliberately sent Henrietta to a school where she believed the supervision was lax and the pupils were allowed too much freedom. The fact that this turned out to be untrue was beside the point. A woman who could do such a thing was not fit to have charge of a young girl—and she did still have charge of Henrietta, remember. During the vacations Henrietta was to go to Brauncing, was she not? Perhaps I might have written to tell the General she was absolutely safe while she was at school, only I knew he had drifted into the habit of evading his responsibilities, and I felt that any reassurance would be made into an excuse for doing nothing."

Thinking it over Honor decided he was right. She knew the General well enough by now to realize what an effort it had been for him to leave his island. Even though he was now rather enjoying himself.

"In any case," she pointed out, "Henrietta was not absolutely safe at school, was she? But there's still something I don't understand."

"The answer ought to be perfectly plain."

"You don't know the question yet."

"Of course I do. You want to know why I never warned you that there was some mystery surrounding Henrietta. Well, how could I? Without explaining what a mean and contemptible part I'd played in the business—injuring your chances of success and abusing you and Lucy, simply to please myself and exact a secret revenge. I was ashamed of what I'd done, especially after I began to fall in love with you. And as I seemed to have a genius for antagonizing you, I hardly felt this confession was going to increase my hopes of marrying you."

He got up and began to walk about the room. Honor was astounded by the suppressed violence of the emotion in his voice.

After a short pause she decided that he was not going to get any further on his own, so she said, "Have you given up your hopes of marrying me?"

He looked at her. "No, my God, I haven't! If you can forgive me—"

"It doesn't matter any more. What are you doing?"

For he had just knocked over a chair.

"Why is there so much genteel furniture in this room?"

"It was meant for school entertainments."

Marcus, who was now kissing her, said, "We never had any entertainment as good as this when I was at school."

They clung together in a state of enraptured bliss which they had both believed unattainable until a few minutes ago. He had been in love with her since the day he rescued her and Nancy from the haberdasher's shop and the threat of transportation. He had felt unable to tell her so until he had tried to undo any harm he might have caused by his malicious gossip to Mrs. Porcheston and his letter to General Delahaye.

They began to remember their former clashes and to compare notes.

"I used to think you quite ugly," said Honor. "How can one be so mistaken?"

"I haven't suddenly grown handsome? Love can't be as blind as that."

"Not handsome precisely," she conceded, gazing into the dark, clever face and the light grey eyes whose mockery had a new tenderness. "But your features are so original and distinguished."

"Very well put! You, on the other hand, have always been enchantingly pretty and I thought so even when you were annoying me most. That was part of the annoyance."

"Lucy knew what was the matter, all along. Oh dear!" she broke off in dismay. "I'd forgotten Lucy."

"What does *oh dear* mean? Lucy will continue with the school, I take it, after we are married? Perhaps she has some friend who could join her?"

"She has a sister who would do splendidly, but where are they to go if we need this house?"

"Do you want to live here?" he asked, surprised. "I thought you would prefer the country."

"Yes, I would. But in that case, shouldn't we have to sell up? I have hardly any other money, you know, and I shall have to settle my debts."

Marcus said thoughtfully, "I don't believe you have ever quite got over your first sight of me in that abominable coat. (I wonder, should I be married in it?) The memory of my shoddy appearance has convinced you that *I* am about to be arrested for debt. Isn't that so?"

"Of course not! Only I know you lost your employment—"

"My what? Oh, you mean my unpaid post at the Embassy. That was never more than a convenience, because I wanted to travel through Turkey and Greece. I have an income which will enable us to live quite comfortably and also keep the school afloat until Lucy has enough pupils to make it a paying concern. That is what you'd like to do, isn't it? Even if it meant a few small economies, like dispensing with a third footman and living in one of those horrid houses where there is no deer park and the breakfast room faces the wrong way?"

When he started talking about footmen and deer parks, she could not be sure how much he was teasing her, whether he had just enough to live on or was in fact a rich man. It hardly seemed to matter, so long as they were able to marry.

"It's very generous of you," she said. "I really think Lucy could succeed here if she isn't bedeviled by money worries."

"I have great faith in Lucy's ability as a teacher. Ever since I heard her speak of reading as a doorway to other worlds. It was at Sally's picnic, and I must have said something flippant, for you thought I was sneering at female education. I suppose I was trying to disguise my true feelings. There was a time when books were all I had to keep me sane. That was when I began working on Homer."

How unhappy his first marriage must have been, she thought. Perhaps in time I shall be able to find out what was wrong. And make it up to him.

"Speaking of Homer," she said. "I'm afraid I haven't read your translation yet—"

"Have you still got it? I was sure you would have thrown it on the kitchen fire in disgust."

"Certainly not! Well, I might have done, if Nancy hadn't asked to borrow it. And she has painted a most dramatic picture of the Trojan Horse."

Marcus immediately asked to see this masterpiece. It was on the wall of the little schoolroom next door, and Honor took him in there to see it.

"It certainly is a very spirited composition," he said, laughing... "And she has given the Horse such a sly expression. I like that."

They were standing by the window now, and looking out she saw the little group on the opposite pavement, coming rather wearily up the hill. The three younger girls, Sally, Evelina and Marianne seemed cheerful enough.

"... 'Regardless of their doom, the little victims play,'" quoted Marcus.

"Sally's doom is to have me as a stepmother," said Honor, thinking: dear Sally, what a delightful ready-made daughter to start our family.

The slightly older victims were not so lighthearted. Nancy scowling as she stumped along, Martha and Margaret oddly forlorn in the faded dresses which they were both growing out of, Lucy looking as Honor remembered her at Walbury the day Euphemia dismissed her. They had probably made the most of their visit to the labyrinth and kept up their spirits; now that was over, Lucy and the older girls had all fallen silent, fearful of the future for their different reasons and unable to go on pretending. An hour ago, Honor could not have endured the pain of watching them.

Now she could hardly wait for them to cross the road and come into the house, so that they could each have their share in her great happiness.

Let COVENTRY Give You
A Little Old-Fashioned Romance

CURRENT BESTSELLERS
from POPULAR LIBRARY